THE

OF FROST

A NOVELLA IN THE HAUNTED SERIES

TONY
MARTURANO

a Different Angle

Published in the United Kingdom and the rest of the world by a Different Angle 2024
Cambridge, UK

A catalogue record for this book is available from the British Library

ISBN - 978-1-0685052-0-1

A NOTE FROM ME

I was already wrestling with the deadline for *Nemesis* when the producers of Dr. NoSleep Studios – makers of the world's #1 horror podcast – reached out. They asked if I'd write an original horror story for Halloween. My first thought? 'Are you kidding me?' I love a challenge, but juggling two simultaneous short deadlines?

But then I started thinking... Writing a novel takes time, of course – but what about a short story? I might just be able to pull this off. But it couldn't be just any story. If I did this, it had to be intense, terrifying, and part of something larger.

If the first three books in the *Haunted* series (known as the origin trilogy) dive deep into Marco Battista's character and the supernatural horrors surrounding him – and *Nemesis* (book four of the series) moves beyond that by introducing Marco to other terrifying stories from around the globe, then what happened the year before the events of *Nemesis*, after Frost Lake Manor was sold? Did the new owners go on to live a happy and prosperous life, or was there some truth to the rumours of the place being cursed?

The Curse of Frost Lake Manor doesn't just answer those questions, it forms a bridge between the supernatural horror of the *Haunted* series and the satanic terror of the *Sinister* series. For those eagle-eyed readers who've spotted Easter eggs in my previous books, you're in for a treat. This is where the two series finally converge in one universe.

So, whether you're here to uncover what happened after *Cursed* or simply seeking a standalone ghost story, I hope you enjoy *The Curse of Frost Lake Manor* as much as I loved writing it.

And if you haven't yet listened to the original podcast edition and enjoyed those inimitable shivers down your spine, check it out now on YouTube or via your favourite podcast streamer. Alternatively, if you're new to the *Haunted* and *Sinister* series, there's plenty of time to scare yourself silly. Catch up now, both are available on Amazon.

Oh, one last thing: however you choose to experience this story, be sure to lock your doors and windows. You know, just as a precaution. You never know what might be lurking out there…

With terror,

Tony

"To kończy się dla ciebie."
(It ends for you.)

SUNDAY

The seatbelt sign dings, and the intercom crackles to life. A polished British accent fills the cabin.

Ladies and gentlemen, this is your captain speaking. We'll be starting our descent into London Heathrow shortly. The local time is 7:15 AM, and the weather on the ground is bright and sunny, though a chilly 12 degrees Celsius – that's 53 Fahrenheit. Please ensure your seatbelts are fastened. Thank you for flying with us, and we hope you enjoy your stay in London. Flight attendants, prepare for landing.

I shift in my seat, pulse quickening. So this is it. It's really happening.

It's been just a few days, and I still can't believe it, which is probably why I barely slept on the flight. Maybe I'm already dreaming... or having a nightmare. Depends how you look at it.

Senior Executive of Property Acquisitions for the Karlson Hotel Group. I've been repeating it to myself ever since Jackson Anderson, VP of Property Acquisitions, announced my promotion at Friday's impromptu meeting.

If it weren't for Aunt Elsie, I would never have helped Mr Jensen sell his place when he decided to retire. Negotiating – I didn't know the meaning of the word back then, but Aunt Elsie always said I had a way with words. She insisted that the place didn't sell because of a hard sell, but because I cared. By explaining what Mr Jensen's dairy farm meant to our community, I gave it personality. Elsie believed in me, even when I didn't.

And when our apple orchard was struggling because we couldn't compete and I started looking at jobs as a farmhand, it was Elsie who said she wouldn't hear of it. She berated Mr Miller until he gave me my first job at Miller & Sons Realtors.

The commission from that job helped us stay afloat until I came home one afternoon to find Aunt Elsie lying on that cold kitchen floor... I couldn't stay there. Selling the farm was probably my worst deal ever, but it meant I could leave the place debt-free to start anew. Mr Miller gave me a recommendation for a realtor in the city, and when I saw the advertisement for the position at Karlson Properties, it was he who encouraged me to apply – he said I was destined for great things.

It wasn't easy. Being a country boy from the small town of Elmswood, Iowa, in the big city has its own handicap, but I kept my mouth shut and head down to the grindstone. Just like Elsie always said. And I was happy. I never in a million years would have expected this.

The Karlson Group... one of the largest conglomerates in the world. They own everything – hotels, real estate, brands you see everywhere. And my job? Find new properties with potential. Not just to make money but to outmanoeuvre the competition. It's a whole different world from where I started. Realtors usually focus on selling high; we're about buying low. Sounds glamorous, but it's cutthroat. The biggest deals are reserved for the top dogs – like Eric Parker. I was, well, a junior by comparison.

So yeah, it's gonna take a while to wrap my head around the fact that Anderson fired him and then handed me his job. Everyone gasped when they heard – hell, I did too. And then they laughed. Of course, I laughed right along with them because, well, it had to be a joke, right?

But no. With Anderson, nothing's a joke. That man, with his three-piece suits and no-bullshit attitude, can command a room with just a look. All he had to do was scowl, and the whole place went dead quiet.

You could hear a pin drop.

What the fuck?

It didn't make sense. I mean, I know, Aunt Elsie would be all over this, spouting sayings like *Don't go looking a gift horse in the mouth.* Hell, it didn't make sense to David "The Hammer" Harris either. He's been at Karlson longer than I have and is way more experienced. Which kind of explained why he cornered me in the men's room shortly after and wanted to know whose dick I sucked to land—

"Sir? Sir?" I blink and look up to see a flight attendant with meticulously painted eyes and hair neatly wrapped in a bun. She's watching me closely. There's a moment of confusion before she says, "Please, sir, your seatbelt."

"Oh, right. Yeah, sorry," I mutter, grabbing the two pieces and clicking them together.

I glance out the window, and for a moment, I'm caught by the view. Clouds – a whole mountain range of them – scattered across the sky. Below, glimpses of the English countryside stretch out like a patchwork quilt, vibrant greens woven together like a painter's dream. Back home in Elmswood, the fields are gold or brown, especially in the summer. But here, the green rolls on forever, lush forests and meadows, endless and alive.

As the engine's roar fades and we descend, the landscape sharpens. Small houses appear, neatly clustered, like tiny toys perfectly arranged along winding roads cutting through the greenery. I've landed in another world, so far removed from my own that my excitement turns to queasiness, twisting my gut.

I take a deep breath. Never thought I'd leave the States, let alone fly across the Atlantic for a job like this. The countryside stretches out below, vast but somehow intimate, like it belongs in a painting. The contrast to home is striking – everything feels so different yet strangely familiar.

The plane judders as we approach the ground, the cabin suddenly quiet. The buildings outside grow larger, and then the wheels touch down with a gentle thud. The engines roar again, pressing me back into my seat before settling into the hum of the air conditioning.

There's a smattering of applause. For a second, I consider joining in. I don't.

The intercom crackles to life again. *Ladies and gentlemen, welcome to London Heathrow. The local time is...*

I'm here. I'm really here.

It takes about an hour to get through immigration and baggage claim and what feels like another hour at the rental kiosk. Eventually, I head for the exit, juggling my rental agreement and baggage. Stepping into the cool, crisp air, the scent of car fumes and the bustle of people hit me. But the weather – it's nothing like the drizzle I expected. Instead, it's a bright, sunny day under a clear, pale blue sky. The sun barely warms the air, but I welcome it.

I pause, letting the sunlight touch my face as I listen to the surrounding accents – accents I've never heard before, but I kind of like them. It keeps me entertained as I ride the shuttle through the airport's maze, passing terminals and parking lots until we finally reach the rental car lot.

I spot my rental – a blue Golf – right where it's supposed to be. The steering wheel? Not so much. It's on the opposite side.

I blink, half-expecting it to shift back to where it belongs, but of course, it doesn't. I knew this was coming, but seeing it in person is a whole different story. Taking a deep breath, I walk around to the driver's side – well, the British driver's side – and toss my bags on the backseat.

With an amused chuckle and a shake of my head, I shrug off my fleece, slide into the driver's seat, and sit there for a moment as my hand instinctively reaches for the gear stick that's now on my left. I adjust the rearview mirror. My reflection stares back at me: dark circles under grey eyes that usually look blue, but not today. My hair, still brown, at least – no signs of grey yet – looks dishevelled, like I haven't slept in days. Which, to be fair, I haven't.

"Okay, Kevin. You've got this."

I tap on the GPS, punch in the address for the New Forest, and wait for it to do its thing. Instantly, I'm greeted by a voice – smooth, soft, and unmistakably British, the kind you hear narrating documentaries. *The route is being calculated*, the Emma Thompson soundalike informs me before calmly adding, *Take the next left*. After a couple of gear scrunches, I manage to comply, piloting the vehicle out of the parking lot and onto the main road, all while continuously reminding myself: *Left side of the road. Left side! LEFT SIDE!*

The exit from Heathrow is a maze of signs and lanes, each one more confusing than the last. I make a wrong turn almost immediately, ending up in a lane to God knows where. Cars zoom past me, and I can practically feel the heat of the driver's glares.

I grit my teeth and swerve back into the correct lane, narrowly avoiding a bus that honks angrily as it overtakes me. My heart, hammering in my chest, calls time out on this rollercoaster ride.

Finally, I spot the signs for the M25, the highway that'll take me around London and into the countryside. I merge onto it, gripping the wheel so tightly my knuckles are white. Traffic is heavy – cars, trucks, and buses, all moving faster than I'm comfortable with.

I glance at the satnav screen. "M25? M23? *Why do all the roads sound like weapons?!"*

After what feels like an eternity, the motorway starts to thin out. I finally exit onto a smaller road, the concrete jungle giving way to open fields and rolling hills, my death grip on the steering wheel easing.

I take a deep breath and glance out the window. The English countryside is something else – fields dotted with sheep, hedgerows stretching on forever, and quaint little cottages that look like they were pulled straight from a fairy tale. It's peaceful, and for the first time since I landed, I start to relax.

The New Forest National Park covers 566 square kilometres of untouched woodland, heathland, and river valleys. Deer, horses, ponies, cattle, and an array of wildlife roam freely in this haven. It was established by William the Conqueror, the first Norman king of England, in 1079. That detail from my research into this place has stayed with me.

Frost Lake Manor is at the centre of this haven. The history alone will be enough to draw people here year-round, but I know that if I play this right, the success of this property could put me on the map, literally. *I can't – I won't screw this up.*

The GPS tells me to take the next left, and I do, finding myself on an even smaller, winding road. It's almost enjoyable now – the quiet hum of the engine, the moving scenery. But as I venture deeper into the countryside, I realise something – there's no actual sign of the New Forest. Not on the road, not on the satnav.

You've reached your destination, Emma suddenly announces.

I glance at the screen. "What?" I look around, but all I see are fields and trees. "Great." In my rush to escape London, I'd entered New Forest as the destination, but this place is massive. I could be anywhere.

"Shit."

I keep driving. Slowly now, my leisurely countryside drive has suddenly taken a different turn. Great, now I'm reminded of those films where hapless travellers end up taking a wrong turn – for the horrifying.

I glance at the fuel gauge. Half a tank left.

Okay. I'm okay.

I reach for my phone on the passenger seat, keeping my eyes on the road. *No signal.*

"Shit."

I toss the phone back, then keep following the winding road for another five minutes, mulling over my situation. The New Forest has been beautiful and all, but the solitude is starting to wear on me. Then, I round a bend and spot a small wooden sign: FAWNDALE. POPULATION 313.

"Finally!" Relief floods through me because the place sounds familiar. What's even better is that after what feels like an eternity of empty roads, I spot the first sign of humanity: a lone figure up ahead. They're kneeling by the side of the road, back to me, tending to something on the grassy verge.

I slow the car to a crawl and buzz down the window. Cold, fresh air rushes in, purifying the stale cabin, and I take a moment to breathe it in before clearing my throat. "Excuse me," I say. The person doesn't react, just keeps digging – or whatever they're doing. I try again. "Excuse me?"

Still no response. Just the rhythmic movement of their shoulders.

I roll the car a little closer, considering honking the horn, but I don't want to startle them. I need their help.

"Excuse me!" I call, louder this time, but when they still don't respond, I pull the car to a stop and engage the brake.

Yeah, this whole thing is starting to feel a little creepy. Not just because I'm out here in the middle of nowhere. But hey, it's not exactly *American Werewolf in London* out here, or in this case, the New Forest.

You're about to find out.

I step out; the gravel crunching underfoot as the door pulls itself shut with a firm thud behind me. A cold wind blows down the road, chasing dried leaves and whining through the naked branches of nearby trees, making me shiver. I approach slowly, eyes fixed on the figure's shoulders as they move back and forth – furiously at work, digging, or something.

The light shifts, and I glance up as giant dark clouds smother the sunlight, sending shadows gliding across the landscape. And now, if I'm perfectly honest, things are feeling a little off. I seriously consider heading back to the car.

Safety?

My gut twists as I get closer. I can see it now—the person is dressed in a long, tattered black coat, like something from another century, with a wide-brimmed hat.

"Hello?" I say again, my voice trembling.

Still no response. Just that relentless movement of the shoulders.

I'm about five feet away now, close enough to notice the stiffness in their limbs, the odd angle of their head. Something's not right. Are they having a seizure?

My heart is knocking on my chest, urging me to leave. Now.

I glance back at the car, then at the figure kneeling in the grass. "Ex... excuse me..." Blood pounds in my ears. I take a deep breath and reach out with a trembling hand, fingers brushing against the coarse fabric of the coat before I place a hand on their broad shoulder and—

A flurry of feathers explodes upward, a harsh caw splitting the air. I jump back with a yelp, stumble, and crash into the grass, screaming – a high-pitched screech that doesn't even sound like me – as the crow flaps away overhead.

"JESUS CHRIST!"

I scramble into a sitting position and freeze, staring into a grotesque face. Patches of skin made from sun-bleached straw are clumsily sutured together, pulled taut over a misshapen skull. One eye socket gapes, dark and empty, while the other holds a single, bulging carrot – its orange hue jarring against the pallid straw. A jagged line of tiny carrot teeth forms a twisted grimace, frozen in a silent scream.

A scarecrow. The stench of damp earth and mildew fills my nostrils, mingling with the faint, sweet rot of decaying vegetables.

"SHIT!" I gasp, gawking at the weathered decay twisted into a mockery of a human face. I can see now that its head is attached to a pole, the base hidden in the grass. That's why it swivelled around to face me, the long coat flapping in the breeze, straw poking from its sleeves.

Who the hell would create something like this? Kneeling in the grass like it's about to be executed.

I jump to my feet, heart still thumping in my chest, while the crow and its friends eye me from a nearby tree, their stares almost judgmental.

I blow out a breath. "Sorry."

Another gust of icy wind pushes a clutch of dried leaves to their graves before shoving me against the car like some kind of omen, making me feel like I shouldn't be here. The inkblot of dark clouds staining the once-blue sky only adds to that feeling. I wonder... then shake it off. I'm here for a reason. My career – my credibility – depends on this. I have to make this place work. But first, I have to find it.

Back in the car, I check my phone for a signal. Nothing. Of course. This place is in the back ass of nowhere. That's what's so great about it... Kind of.

"Shit," I sigh, leaning back in my seat. I can't exactly turn back – I'll run out of fuel.

I start the engine, push the car into gear, and move forward, glancing at the scarecrow in the rearview mirror, half expecting the damn thing to move. It doesn't, of course. I'm just freaking myself out.

Get your shit together!

But I've barely made it a few yards when I spot something ahead – a figure standing motionless at the edge of the trees. My grip tightens on the steering wheel, pulse quickening again. The figure comes into focus – another scarecrow, this one standing tall, its head twisted at an unnatural angle as if watching the road. It's dressed in a long black cloak, with equally long hair hanging over its face, hiding the features beneath.

What the fuck?

I shiver as I drive past, the eerie figure looming over the road like some kind of grim reaper. Then, as I round the next bend, I see another – this one even more twisted, wearing a cracked, grotesque mask. One eye is painted in mocking, bloody red, while the other is gouged out entirely. Shit. It's like something out of a slasher movie.

I step on the accelerator, needing to put distance between me and these macabre figures, but they keep coming. On both sides of the road now, scarecrows emerge from the shadows, each more disturbing than the last. Some are traditional, with faded overalls and straw hats, but others are downright terrifying – grinning skull masks, faces covered in burlap with crude, stitched-on smiles, even one with a mannequin's head where its own should be, its glassy eyes staring blankly ahead.

And then I notice them – the houses. Most are small, made of stone and weathered by time. Some have thatched roofs, others are draped in creeping ivy. But there are larger, more imposing ones too, each with its own macabre figure out front.

One figure in particular catches my eye – a short, stooped form dressed in a Victorian shawl with long, wiry grey hair. Some kind of witch, maybe? There's a small white card pinned to the bottom of her shawl. The number 13 flaps in the breeze as golden leaves swirl and tumble to their eternal resting place around her.

I slow the car, leaning forward for a better look. There's something unsettling about the figure, the way it stands there, almost too lifelike, making my skin crawl. Then, suddenly, the witch's head snaps in my direction, looking right at me.

"FUCK!" I gasp, slamming on the brakes. The car lurches to a stop, pressing me into the seatbelt, my breath coming in short, panicked bursts. I crane my neck, staring at the figure, white knuckles gripping the steering wheel. But after blinking, I see she's motionless. Looking closer... it's obvious she didn't move at all. Just another lifeless decoration in the autumn air.

"Shit, Kev. What's the deal?" My heart's throbbing in my chest, and even though that thing isn't moving – except for the wind pushing and pulling at it – I still can't shake the feeling of being watched.

Hastily, I release the brake and let the car roll forward. Up ahead, another stone building comes into view with a large hand-painted sign above the front door –FAWNDALE POST OFFICE AND STORE. Outside, crates brimming with fresh vegetables sit on display, along with an A-board advertising the *FAWNDALE SCARECROW FESTIVAL – Voting forms inside!* I let out a chuckle, along with a sigh of relief. "Of course it is." What I thought was a gauntlet of horror is just a friggin' contest.

I could pull over and ask for directions, but something tells me I'm close. So I keep driving, passing more elaborately decorated contestants as the road narrows again. Before I know it, I'm at the other end of the village, the kind of place you wouldn't even notice if not for the horror fest.

I spot a narrow drive up ahead, partially hidden by overhanging branches. *Could this be it?* Without thinking, I glance in the rearview mirror and veer left onto the gravel, leaves swirling around the tires. Thick trees flank the path, their branches forming a canopy, casting dappled shadows that blur the line between road and forest. The further I go, the colder the air in the car feels – the only sound the crunch and pop of tires on gravel.

I grip the steering wheel tighter – maybe this is one of those wrong turns after all. The car seems to agree as the headlights flick on automatically, the shadows deepening around me.

I glance at the GPS, but it's useless now – a blank screen where the directions should be.

Just as I'm thinking about turning around – though it wouldn't be easy – the trees begin to thin, the road slopes upward, and suddenly, I emerge into a clearing.

The light here is different – golden and soft in patches as the sun slips behind the wall of trees. And then I see it, up ahead. A lawn, a garden, a driveway, and then—

I bring the car to an abrupt stop, letting it idle as tree branches sway around me, shedding leaves that drift and tumble, catching the light one last time before hitting the ground and the windshield. It should be beautiful, but instead, that cold knot of dread tightens in my stomach. For a moment, I just sit here, staring out the windshield, trying to make sense of what I'm seeing. Because if I'm seeing this right... this trip, my career – it's over before it's even started.

Oh, no. This can't be. It can't.

I kill the engine, fumble for the handle, and push the door open, stepping onto the uneven ground. The first thing to hit me is the smell—a pungent mix of burnt wood, damp earth, and the lingering scent of smoke that clings to the wind, suffocating me.

I cough, but it's not from anything I've inhaled. It's more like my body's trying to expel the cold truth sinking in.

The wind picks up, rustling leaves that click and hiss, stirring ashes into swirling patterns around me. Birds sing in the surrounding woodland, indifferent to the tragedy here. My shoes crunch against the blackened earth as I take in the scene before me.

Oh, what the hell happened?

Before me are the charred remains of a house. The roof has collapsed inward, and the walls, reduced to skeletal remnants, are barely standing.

Charred beams lie scattered like broken ribs, twisted metal frames – maybe from balconies or windows – half-buried in the debris. Everything is covered in a thick layer of ash. What must have been a grand estate looks so much smaller than the images suggested.

"I'm finished..." I breathe, a cold chill running down my spine.

I step closer, unable to believe my eyes, but my foot sinks into a pile of ash, nearly sending me sprawling. I catch myself on what's left of a wall, the surface rough and splintered under my fingers. My eyes trace the jagged edge, following it down until they snag on a blackened shape. Leaning in, I brush away the soot to reveal the faint outline of letters: HOLT.

The destruction is total, yet beyond the ruins, something catches my eye. A flash of silver. I take a few steps sideways and realise it's a lake, shimmering through the funeral pyre of broken timbers, eerily calm, reflecting the darkening sky.

Circling the ruins, I find a narrow path leading to the back garden, now overgrown and tangled with weeds. The grass is scorched in places; the earth blackened and bare. Rows of chairs – some toppled, others charred and melted – stand as twisted, distorted forms. Tattered sashes flutter weakly in the breeze, ghostly remnants of a wedding celebration that ended in tragedy. Conversely, the birdsong continues all around, indifferent to it all.

I stand rooted to the spot, my heart heavy with a mix of emotions. This isn't Frost Lake Manor. It can't be. This is something else – a tragedy I wasn't meant to witness.

A sudden shriek startles me, and for a moment, I think it's a survivor emerging from the ruins. But the sound comes from the lake, where a pair of swans takes off from the water's edge, their wings beating furiously, sending ripples across the surface. They rise into the air, their pale feathers catching the last light like ghosts escaping the charred ruins behind me.

I watch them glide away, my gaze drawn to the shimmering reflection on the lake. And then I see it – a massive structure looming in the distance on the opposite shore.

Frost Lake Manor.

I imagine that the only way to get to it from here is through the woods, on foot, but I decide against it. Climbing back into the car, I drive out through the trees.

I stop at the empty road, checking for oncoming traffic, but mostly to gather my thoughts. I don't know what exactly happened back there; all I know is I feel so much better now that I'm back on the empty main road. Lighter. As if some heavy shroud has been lifted off me.

Frost Lake Manor is about a mile down the road, and it's everything befitting an estate of its kind. Twin stone pillars flank the entrance, each topped with a meticulously carved lion's head, their eyes seeming to watch me as I approach. A wrought-iron gate, freshly painted a deep, glossy black, stands open – welcoming, yet imposing.

Above the gate, an elegant sign arches gracefully between the pillars, the words FROST LAKE MANOR etched in gold leaf against a dark green enamel backdrop. The letters gleam in the fading light, catching my eye as I turn off the main road.

The entrance is bordered by low stone walls that stretch out on either side, lined with perfectly trimmed hedges that guide the eye toward the driveway beyond. A pair of lanterns, black and gold, hang from the pillars, flickering to life as evening approaches, casting a warm, inviting glow.

As I pass through the gates, the car jolts over occasional potholes as the road winds through thick woodland. The branches of ancient oaks and elms twist together, forming an almost tunnel-like canopy that makes me grip the steering wheel a little tighter.

Then, through breaks in the trees, I catch my first glimpse of the mansion. It stands imposingly, slowly revealing itself as I navigate the bends in the driveway. The building is massive, a Tudor–Victorian structure perched on a hill overlooking the vast expanse of land. Its ashlar stone walls are weathered but resilient, clinging to the elegance of a bygone era. The pitched slate roof adds a stately presence, with towering chimneys stretching toward the sky. I can't help but admire the craftsmanship – the chisel-dressed stone, the intricate detailing around the windows, and the solid oak doors standing guard under the porte-cochere, an old carriage porch that adds a touch of historical charm.

I pull into the walled courtyard and bring the car to a stop, cutting the engine. Silence envelops me, broken only by the ticking of the cooling engine. I sit there, overwhelmed by an immense sense of accomplishment.

I'm here. At fucking last!

I take a deep breath, feeling suddenly fatigued but overjoyed to have made it. Then I pull on the door handle and step out to the sound of evening birdsong – wood pigeons, crows, and a chorus of others I don't recognise. The front lawn rolls gently down toward the lake. The grass is neatly trimmed, and the pathways look like they've been recently raked, adding to the sense that the place has seen some recent care despite its solitude.

A bitterly cold wind swirls around me, whistling through unseen wires with an eerie whine. It chases the last of the autumn leaves, corralling them into rustling heaps against the base of the stone walls. As the wind settles down, a woodland quiet descends, broken only by the gentle lapping of the lake against the dock's wooden planks. The water, eerily calm now, reflects the deepening twilight. Beyond its dark surface, I can barely make out the charred remains of the place I now know was called Holt.

I can't help but wonder if there's any connection to the manor. It wasn't mentioned in any of the documentation, yet I can't shake the feeling that the two places are linked.

I shiver, brushing away the thought, and turn to face the building. It's magnificent! And yes, I'm fanboying hard here. But come on, a porte-cochère! I think the only other place I've seen one of those is Buckingham Palace.

The double oak doors are freshly stained, their part-glazed panels gleaming in the dim light – evidence of recent attention.

I take a deep breath. The air is fresh, heavy with the scent of damp earth and decaying leaves. It's invigorating, wiping away my weariness as I walk slowly toward the entrance, my footsteps crunching on the gravel. The mansion's size is overwhelming, the sheer scale of it making me feel small. This is it – the place I've been sent to salvage, the place that could make or break my career.

As I approach the door, something catches my eye – strips of yellow tape fluttering in the wind. Police tape. The words are faded, but the instruction remains clear: POLICE—DO NOT CROSS. The tape clings obstinately to the edges of the doorway, rustling and snapping in the wind, a silent testament to the events that transpired here not long ago.

My heart skips a beat. I try to tell myself this is just another property. I've managed plenty before, but something about this one feels different. It feels... occupied, as if unseen tenants are watching, waiting beyond the dark glass of the windows, biding their time.

Seriously, dude? Why don't you wait a little longer until it's dark? Then you can really scare yourself shitless!

The door handle is cold beneath my fingers, the metal loop heavy as I twist it, expecting it to be locked – I'm supposed to be meeting the agent tomorrow. But to my surprise, it swings open with a creak; the sound echoing through the vast space beyond. I hesitate, but then again, contracts have been exchanged; we own this place now. So, I step inside, and the first thing that strikes me is the light – or rather, the lack of it.

The entrance hall is dim, with the last rays of the setting sun barely reaching through the shattered remains of the giant lantern roof above. Where there once might have been a cascade of daylight flooding the room, there's now only the pale, dying light of an autumn evening struggling to penetrate the gloom. The air inside is colder than I expected, a damp chill clinging to my skin.

Looking up, I see why. What should be the centrepiece of the mansion's grandeur is now a gaping wound in the ceiling. Large shards of glass litter the floor, glinting weakly. Someone has tried to cover the hole with a tarp, but it's poorly secured. Now, it flaps loudly in the wind, snapping like a firecracker, echoing around the space and making me jump.

The floor beneath the broken glass is wet in places with puddles forming where rain has leaked through, pooling under a mound of dried leaves. The damp has crept back in, carrying with it the smell of wet stone, decaying wood, and... something else. Something that—*Slam!*

"SHIT!"

Just a door. Just a goddamn door. Somewhere in the gloom, followed by a demonic moan as the wind prowls through the house, trying to reclaim its dominion.

I hastily pull my phone from my pocket. There's still some light, but not enough to shake the unsettling feeling crawling over me like the cold. A couple of taps and the LED light flickers to life. I take a few steps forward, my shoes crunching on scattered glass, and take in the scene.

Doors flank me on the left and right, and the once-pristine floor that Marco – the former owner – and his team restored after years of neglect is now marred by recent damage. Water and glass glint among the dirt and debris, and even a few stray weeds are taking root, as if nature is reclaiming its territory.

Directly ahead, the grand split staircase rises to a landing dominated by a giant grandfather clock, its age showing. The banister splits left and right to the first-floor galleries, darkened in places from moisture. High above, the walls still hold, though water stains and streaks have crept in, probably looking worse in daylight.

A creaking sound draws my attention to the left of the staircase. I move forward, the light beam revealing the ornate detail of the banister, the wall, and... a smaller-than-average door built into the side of the staircase. The cellar? That's what I imagine. The door creaks in some invisible draft, and I consider going over to push it shut when a loud screech makes me jump. I lose my footing on the debris and crash backward onto the floor, my phone carving wild shapes out of the gloom before clattering nearby.

"SHIT!"

I've barely got my bearings when movement overhead catches my eye – just in time to see a patch of white gliding over me like a ghost!

"FUCK!"

I scramble for my phone, aiming it upward like a weapon, revealing a pair of giant circular eyes staring at me from the gallery balustrade.

SCREECH!

The sound rakes down my last nerve before I finally process what I'm seeing. "Shit," I breathe, my heart pounding in my chest.

It's an owl. A fucking owl. Must've come in through the open roof.

"Hey, fella. You're trespassing," I mutter, voice shaky. The bird just stares at me, unflinching, and suddenly, it's me who feels like the intruder.

"Ow..." My palm stings. I shine the light on it to see a rivulet of blood dripping from a shard of glass embedded in my skin, glinting in the LED light.

I sigh and pluck it out, wincing as a few more drops of blood follow. Then – movement. My light swings across the room, but there's nothing. I aim the beam upward – the owl is still on its perch. Back down again –

just that open cellar door and shadows.

"Seriously?"

The haunted house trope isn't lost on me, and I half chuckle, expecting the door to slam shut. When it does, the bang is so loud it scares my feathered friend from its perch, sending it fluttering up and out through the hole in the roof. I immediately follow suit – irrational, maybe – but I've had enough creepy British shit for one day.

I don't even look back as I run out of the door to the car – after heading to the wrong side first, of course – and get the hell out of there.

So, okay, maybe not my finest hour, but looking on the bright side, there was nobody there to witness me hightailing it except that owl. And I doubt he's going to tell anyone.

As part of my research, I found a B&B near the manor, ironically called the Stag & Owl. It's a cosy little pub with a thatched roof and ivy clinging to its walls.

By the time I reach the outskirts of the village, dark clouds gather overhead, spitting the first drops of rain onto my windshield. It quickly turns into a steady downpour, followed by freezing rain, the wipers barely keeping up.

I'm relieved when the pub sign appears through the downpour, even if pulling into the gravel lot feels a bit like a scene at the Bates Motel. But I'm too tired to care. Besides, the place is inviting, its old-world charm radiating from the leaded windows casting warm, golden light into the dark evening – a sharp contrast to where I've just come from.

I park under the illuminated pub sign, grab my bag, and summon enough energy to make a mad dash for the entrance, shielding myself from the freezing deluge.

Inside, the warmth hits me like a wall. A fire crackles in the hearth, and the landlord, Danny – a skinny guy with a sleeve tattoo and a grin that says he's seen it all – greets me like I'm an old buddy. The place is small but welcoming, with low wooden beams and a bar that's clearly served many a pint. The smell of fried food, beer, and woodsmoke fills the air, and my stomach growls on cue. Lucky for me, it's fish and chip night, served up in a rustic basket and washed down with a beer and some small talk about where I'm from.

I keep the reason for my visit on the down-low – for now. I'm exhausted and not ready to dive into the whole what-happened-there thing.

Thankfully, it isn't long before Danny offers to show me to my room upstairs. It's up its own narrow flight of stairs and feels more like an attic than a regular room, small but clean and comfortable with a thick quilt on the bed and heavy curtains drawn tight against the cold night.

The rain's really coming down now, hammering against the skylight like a drumline. I'm worn out – full belly and beer doing a good job of smoothing out the day's rough edges – but I resist the urge to collapse onto the tiny bed and head for the shower instead.

The hot water is a godsend, the warmth sinking into my bones and washing away the chill that's clung to me since the manor. After what feels like forever, I step out, dry off, and slide under the covers, pulling them up to my chin. The rhythmic percussion of the rain against the skylight lulls me, and before I know it, I'm drifting off into a deep, delicious sleep.

The next thing I know, my eyes snap open. I turn, hand groping the nightstand until my fingers brush against my glasses. The digital clock glares red in the darkness – 3:13 AM. I blink at the numbers, my brain foggy with sleep. A cold knot tightens in my stomach; something about the time feels off.

I roll over, pulling the covers tighter around me, trying to dismiss the unease as leftover stress from the day.

It's cold in here, and just as I consider braving the chill to check the thermostat, I hear it – a creak on the landing outside my room.

I freeze, every muscle tense. It's the kind of creak that's too deliberate, too specific, too loud just to be the house settling... *Did I lock the door?*

I strain my ears, the blood pounding in my temples. The rain continues its steady drumming on the skylight, filling the silence, but beneath it is something else. My eyes snap to the narrow strip of light that's appeared under the door. The stair light, activated by a motion sensor, has flicked on. It's the only source of light in the otherwise pitch-black hallway.

I stare at it. I'm the only one up here. There's no reason for anyone else to be out there. *Who would be? Why?*

My breath catches when a shadow suddenly falls across the light beneath the door. My body tenses.

There's someone out there.

I sit up slowly, heart racing, every instinct screaming at me to be still, to listen, to calm down. Any second now, Danny the landlord is going to knock on the door, apologise for disturbing me, and tell me that—

Creak!

Another creak. There's definitely somebody out there, standing outside my door.

Rain raps against the skylight as I realise I'm still holding my breath, tension building in my skull, blood ringing in my ears.

"Hello?" The word slips out with trapped air as I breathe in short bursts, trying to hear through the drone of the rain.

And then – the light flicks off. No more shadow, but I'm lucid enough now to know that doesn't mean whoever's out there is gone. It just means they could still be there, standing perfectly still.

I'm processing this terrifying thought, debating my next move, when the wind, frustrated by its failed attempts to breach the building, throttles the swinging sign outside, making it squeal like a wounded animal before moving onto the skylight and threatening to tear it off its hinges.

I rub my face, trying to shake off the chill crawling down my spine. *It's fine. It's okay.* It was probably just a cat out there. And yet, I'm still listening, straining through the rain for something – anything – that doesn't belong.

Nothing.

"Shit..." I hiss under my breath, turning over and settling back down into the bed, forcing myself to relax, even though I can't seem to rip my eyes from the outline of the door.

It's just a storm. Just the weather. It's nothing compared to Tornado Alley. Get a grip!

But the unease clings to me like the cold in this room. Fear. I'm afraid, and I don't even know why.

Tap! Tap!

The skylight! It's probably ivy. And yet, despite the limited visibility, I'm still staring at it, half expecting a pair of malevolent eyes to appear at any moment.

Seriously? You're supposed to be a grown-ass man. There's nothing out there. Just the weather. Just the rain... and that demon wind!

It howls around the building, moaning through the eaves.

Tap... tap... tap. Rain on the window? No, it didn't sound like that. This was different – sharper. Deliberate.

I reach for the bedside lamp, but another *TAP!* stops me. This one's louder. Like something striking the glass. Like someone throwing stones?

I freeze. Wait... listen... Rain falls. Drainpipes gurgle.

I hesitate, wondering if turning on the light is a good idea. I'd be revealing myself.

TAP! TAP! Sharp fingernails tapping at the window now. *Creak, scratch...* at the skylight. *Tap! Creak! Scratch!* The sounds overlap, creating a growing cacophony to rival the storm, my head snapping between noises, hairs prickling all over my body.

Louder.

Faster.

LOUDER!

FASTER! The sounds come from everywhere at once, squeezing my chest with short, shallow breaths, fear boiling over into anger. "NO!" I throw back the covers and leap out of bed, feet hitting the cold floor. I hesitate – heart thundering in my chest – staring at the window.

There's nothing out there. *Is there?*

And yet, I pad over, floorboards creaking under my weight. My breath catches as I get closer, every step pulling me toward whatever might be waiting on the other side of the glass. I take a beat, half-expecting to see something – someone – staring back at me.

But I don't know why I bothered. The window is just a dim rectangle, blurred by rain streaking down the pane. There's nothing out there.

I pause, heart still racing, staring out at the empty parking lot below. The rain is relentless, turning the gravel into a dark, shimmering sea. My eyes are drawn to the illuminated pub sign swinging back and forth as it's roughly manhandled by the wind. It's the only source of light out here. Without it, the countryside would be pitch black – just an endless void.

The light flickers, casting long, eerie shadows across the lot, illuminating my car and the few others parked nearby. I watch as the sign swings back and forth, creating an unsettling dance of shadows on the wet ground.

It's just a rainstorm, I repeat to myself, but my nerves remain taut as the light flickers again, sputtering like it's struggling to stay alive. And then, in one of those strobing moments, I see her.

I jolt back from the window, heart in my throat, but I can't help but look again, an overwhelming sense of dread washing over me. There, standing by my car – a figure, small and hunched, sodden white hair hanging in curtains over her face and falling around her shoulders. The light blinks once more, and just as quickly as she appeared – she's gone.

But it was her! I know it was her – the scarecrow of the old lady.

I hold my breath, trying to focus, trying to see through the rain and the flickering light. But the more I stare, the less sure I am of what I saw. Was it her or just a trick of the light? I press my face closer to the glass, eyes straining to see, but there's nothing out there.

Nothing.

I stay like that for several seconds until I become aware of it – the sudden silence in my room. No tapping. No scratching. Just the hum of the rain until... *creak!*

The sound of someone walking on the floorboards – of someone in my room!

I whirl around, breath frozen in my throat, heart pickaxing against my ribs. The light spilling through the window is barely enough to outline the skeletons of the furniture, but it's enough to see that there's nobody here with me – that I'm alone.

And yet, the throbbing in my chest, the shallow breaths, continue as I become aware of something across the room, something that fills me with a terror so palpable I start to tremble – the door, which I was sure I'd locked, is now wide open. No sound, no warning, just the rectangular black void of the hallway.

I stand there gaping at it, wanting to leap over and slam it shut – but I can't move. I'm rooted in place, paralysed by fear of God knows what, as the air around me shifts, thickens, and condenses into a foul stench of decay and damp earth that claws at my lungs, making me gag.

I fold inward, heaving and spluttering, just fighting the bile rising in my throat when I feel it – so faint at first, I don't even notice. Only when the sensation spreads across my scalp do I become aware of it. A tickle, like insect legs crawling through the roots of my hair.

I open my mouth to scream, but the sound dries in my throat as I reach up – and my fingers meet something cold and slick. Wet strands, clinging to my fingers like tendrils. Oh, my God... that isn't cold water – it's long, sodden strands of hair!

Dread sinks its claws into me as I feel the tendrils creep forward onto my forehead, over my face, brushing against my cheeks as I slowly, ever so slowly, lift my eyes upward.

And I see her!

Hanging upside down from the ceiling like some grotesque, giant arachnid. Her body is contorted, limbs twisted at unnatural angles. Her face is inches from mine – a grotesque mask of mummified flesh, mottled with dark, festering patches where the skin has peeled. Her eyes are sunken pits, the remnants of eyelids peeled back to reveal a milky, dead gaze. Her slash of a mouth – twisted and malformed – hangs open, a black void filled with jagged, broken teeth, yellowed and decaying, jutting out at odd angles like shards of bone.

A guttural, rasping breath escapes her, sending a cold rush of foul air across my face. I want to scream, but my voice is caught in my throat, strangled by the sheer horror of what I'm seeing. Her head tilts, studying me, before that gash of a mouth opens and distends unnaturally wide, as if to swallow me whole.

I scream... and jolt awake!

The rain drums against the skylight, a relentless percussion that merges with the remnants of that hideous nightmare. I sit for several seconds, catching my breath as I gape at the bedroom door.

It's closed.

Only after my brain fully processes this reality do I become aware of the sharp, persistent vibration of my phone on the nightstand. I hastily reach over and snap on the bedside lamp, welcoming the light into the room.

Then I look at the screen of my vibrating phone, which is now travelling across the nightstand like an angry insect. The name JACKSON ANDERSON flashes insistently on the display.

I glance at the time. 04:03.

With a sigh, I pick up the phone and press connect.

"Hello?" I rasp, then promptly clear my throat, my voice rough with sleep.

"Kevin," Anderson's voice drawls through the line, smooth as molasses, with that unmistakable Texas twang. "Hope I didn't catch ya at a bad time."

I sit up, rubbing a hand over my face, trying to shake off the fog of the nightmare still clinging to me like the bedsheets. *Ugh.* "It's, uh, the middle of the night here, sir."

"Is it?" He sounds surprised, as if the time difference is a quaint little detail he hadn't considered. "Well, you know how it is – time waits for no man."

"Sure," I mumble, pulling the cover off me and swinging my legs over the side of the bed. "What, uh, can I do for you, Mr Anderson?"

"Just checkin' in, son. Get a sit rep on progress made so far."

I hesitate, trying to find the right words. "I, uh, only just got here, sir. Haven't really had a chance to—"

"Well, technically, you got in yesterday, your time," he interrupts.

"Yeah, but—"

"Son, do I need to remind you just how important this project is for the brand?"

I swallow, feeling a knot tighten in my gut. "No, sir... of course not."

"I don't have to spell it all out again for ya?"

"No, sir."

"Good, because I don't wanna bother Dave with this. He's already got his hands full in Dubai, and I'd rather not recall him to babysit – but I can if y'all are feelin'... overwhelmed."

Dave "The Hammer" Harding. The nickname isn't just for show. Dave is Anderson's go-to guy – the man who made his name by hammering square pegs into round holes and making it look easy. He's proved time and time again that he can achieve the impossible, no matter the cost. The guy's a machine – driven, relentless – the son Anderson never had and rumoured son-in-law hopeful. If Harding wasn't already busy fixing problems for Anderson on the other side of the world, there's no doubt he'd be here instead of me. But there was nobody else. So here I am. And there's no way in hell I'm letting that hammer fall on me.

There's a pause on the other end of the line, filled by the gentle tap of rain that finally seems to be slowing, along with the throb in my chest.

"I can count on ya then?" Anderson asks, the question purely rhetorical.

"One hundred percent, sir. I won't let you down," I say, resolve finding its way into my voice.

"Good. See that you don't. There's a lot ridin' on this – especially for you," he adds.

I nod, even though he can't see me, my grip tightening on the phone. "Understood."

"Good man. By the way, we're fixin' to have that place ready for New Year's."

My heart skips a beat. "New Year's? But that's—"

"Two months away," he cuts in, voice like steel. "Is there a problem?"

I hesitate, pressure building in my skull as I think of the state of the manor. *Now's your chance! Just be honest.*

Water drips. Drainpipes gurgle.

"No, sir. No problem. We'll be ready."

"Glad to hear it. I'll expect regular updates. Now, get some rest – you're gonna need it." The line goes dead before I can respond.

I lower the phone, staring at it as the call disconnects. But as the screen turns black, the threat of losing my job takes a backseat to my dream, because even now, with the light burning and the shadows banished, I still have this horrible sense of being watched.

MONDAY

I spent what was left of the night drifting in and out of sleep – with the light on, and I'm not ashamed to admit it. Part of me was too tired to care, and the other part... well, let's just leave it at that.

By 07:30, my stomach was grumbling as the smell of a fried breakfast wafted under my perfectly innocent – by day – locked door.

After a shower in a bathroom not much bigger than my closet back home – and I live in a tiny apartment in Washington Heights, though that shithole is nowhere near as rustic – I headed down for breakfast.

It was a *Full English*, or a *fry-up* as the Brits call it: eggs, bacon, sausages, and a strange side order of... baked beans? *Beans? What's that about?*

Other than that little distraction, I spent most of my breakfast tapping an action plan into my phone, along with a list of some of the biggest challenges I'm going to face in getting Frost Lake Manor ready for its grand opening in just two months.

The UK hotel industry is worth nearly thirty billion dollars, and the Karlson Group is desperately trying to carve out a share. The only way to do that is by establishing a dominant presence. Frost Lake Manor is a geographical gem for the corporation. They already missed out on a deal once before – for reasons unknown – under Anderson's watch. It was a huge embarrassment for him, which means this is personal.

And now it's personal for me.

The property itself is in fairly good shape, thanks to all the work that was done before the accident. But based on what I saw yesterday, there are still some major repairs needed – and I haven't even inspected the rest of the building yet. Then there's the obvious remodelling, like the front of house and the structure that goes with it. The list feels endless.

Oh, fuck. I feel queasy just thinking about it. Most of the time, I'd be up for the challenge – it's what got me here in the first place – but this time? Shit, I'm in a foreign country with no crew. I don't even think The Hammer could pull this off. Then again, *Can't never did anything.* That's what Aunt Elsie used to say.

One of the first calls I made this morning was to Kal, the agent who introduced me to Marco Battista – the property developer who owns Frost Lake Manor. We were just weeks away from exchanging contracts before the accident, so I know he's just as eager as I am to close this deal. The problem is he's back in London, convalescing, with no appetite to return here anytime soon. So I made him a proposition. If he goes for it, that'll be the first major obstacle out of the way – just another hundred or so to go in pulling this off.

Kal also lined up a meeting with the contractor for this morning that I need to go well, which is why I'm now dressed in a casual suit and rushing out the door. I need to be at the Manor in exactly ten minutes.

I'm still buttoning up my shirt as I make my way to the stairs when my foot kicks something hard. It rolls down the narrow, creaky wooden steps with a hollow, uneven sound, then keeps going – tumbling all the way down the main flight to the bottom step. "What the hell?" I mutter, peering down.

The object, whatever it is, has rolled to a stop at the base of the staircase. I squint, trying to make sense of it. It's small, about the size of a baseball, but it's not a ball. At least, it doesn't look like one. This is darker, rougher, and seems to be wrapped in something... organic.

I follow it down.

Was that thing outside my room yesterday? I don't remember seeing it. But then again, I was dog-tired.

Reaching the bottom, I bend down, hesitating for a second, tentatively prodding the thing before picking it up. It's heavier than it looks. Ugly, too – close up, it's even worse. It looks like green and yellow vines twisted around—

"Fuck!" I drop the thing. It lands with a loud plop but doesn't roll away. One of the big thorns at its centre just pricked my finger. I shake the pain away, watching as a bead of blood wells up from the tiny wound.

Son of a bitch. It stings. Who'd make something like this?

I walk down the short corridor to the bar. It's empty, but I hear voices coming from what I assume is the kitchen out back. I consider going to the door and knocking, but I'm late. So instead, I grab napkins from the bar and hurry out of the place.

I step outside into a world still dripping from last night's downpour. The sky is a heavy blanket of dark and light grey clouds, like the heavens can't decide whether to open up again or just brood overhead. The air is cold and sharp, biting into my lungs with each breath, a stark contrast to the stale air of New York. For a moment, I feel a pang of something I haven't felt in a long time... homesickness. And by that, I mean Elmswood, not New York. Weird. I don't think I've ever really missed home since I left.

A rusty groaning sound catches my attention. I look up at the pub sign swinging back and forth, its weathered metal protesting against the wind. The rain-soaked memory of last night comes flooding back, sending a shiver down my spine, but I push it aside. I don't have time for this.

Crows caw as I take a deep breath, letting the crisp air clear my head, and walk over to one of the green trash cans I spotted yesterday. I lift the lid, dump the ball – now carefully wrapped in napkins – inside, and let the lid slam shut with a satisfying bang.

The drive to Frost Lake Manor is shorter than I expected, and the mass of grey and black clouds pressing down on the landscape emphasises the sense of isolation. Last night's rain has left the road slick, the tires hissing against the wet asphalt as I navigate the winding roads.

When the trees finally part, revealing the estate, the sight momentarily takes my breath away. Even though I was here yesterday, Frost Lake Manor looks entirely different, bathed in the cool, misty light of morning. The Tudor-Victorian structure looms larger now, its slate roof and tall chimneys piercing through the low-hanging fog like the turrets of a forgotten castle. The sprawling lawns, which seemed so neatly kept before, are now shrouded in mist, giving the landscape an eerie stillness as they slope down to the lake. The water is darker than I remembered, reflecting the stormy sky above and blending with the grey haze that cloaks the scene.

The veil of mist either enhances the beauty of this place or amplifies its sense of foreboding – I can't quite decide. I deliberately avoid glancing toward the far end of the lake, where the charred ruins still sit in ominous silence. The sight of them stirs something deep and unsettling inside me.

As I pull onto the forecourt, something new catches my eye: a battered truck parked near the entrance, with the faded words IRVIN & SONS barely visible on its rusted tailgate. It's a stark contrast to the grandeur of the manor, a reminder that time hasn't been as kind to everything here.

Okay. Not quite what I expected. After all the glowing reports from the agent and Battista himself, I imagined a crew of many with a fleet of sleek trucks. This is nothing like what I had in mind.

I bring the car to a stop behind the truck, my gaze fixed on the scene through the windshield. An older man wearing a flat cap stands flanked by two younger men. I leave the car, forcing a smile as I hunch against the cold blowing leaves from trees.

"Irvin?" I ask, extending a hand to the man in the flat cap.

"That's me," he says, shaking my hand with a firm grip. "You must be Kevin."

"I sure am," I reply, keeping the grin intact as I make a point of glancing at the other two.

Irvin takes the cue. "This is Drew," he says, "and Dean." Drew, tall and lanky with a mop of ginger hair, gives me a nod. Dean, quieter and more reserved, offers a brief smile before his gaze drifts back to the manor.

An awkward pause stretches between us, the silence filled only by the soft cooing of wood pigeons perched somewhere high above. The stillness is so profound it feels like we should be whispering. "Sorry I'm a little late," I say, though the real question itching at the back of my mind is *Where's the rest of your crew? I was expecting more workers. We're never gonna get this place finished in time!*

"Oh, no worries. Was your flight okay?"

"Yes, thanks," I reply, but the conversation stalls again, filled by the distant sound of wings flapping – swans, I think – out on the lake. And then, out of nowhere, I blurt, "Look, Irvin, can I give this to you straight? I know you guys aren't exactly keen on coming back here after... well, after what happened. But your boss and my boss – they're both invested in this.

Your boss wants to unload this place for obvious reasons, and my boss is still interested in taking it off his hands. I need you to help me make that happen. What do you say?"

I finally take a breath, but it might as well be my last because I'm pretty sure I just blew the one tip the agent gave me – don't pressure the guy. He's known not to respond well to that. And here I am, laying it on thick with all this your boss, my boss crap.

Shit.

I watch as Irvin shifts his weight, his expression unreadable as he folds his arms and leans against the truck. "What is it exactly you're needin' us for?"

I'm still recovering from my verbal diarrhoea, leaving me gawking at the guy for way longer than is normal before I manage to string together a response. "Well, um... the... damage... the damp in the lobby."

"What damage exactly?"

I frown. "Did you guys not look inside?" I ask, noticing how all three of them glance at the manor, but their gazes don't linger. It's like they can't bring themselves to really look at the place. Now that I think about it, they haven't even parked outside the front door but some ways off, as if keeping their distance from something they'd rather not face. And I know I'm in trouble. Something about this place has spooked these men. I need to come up with something fast if I don't want to lose them. Yet, every time I try to find the words, they keep disappearing inside the fog of my headache. I open my mouth to speak but stop when I notice the trio looking over my shoulder.

I turn to follow their gaze to the treeline, and there's no doubt in my mind – it's one of those Hollywood moments where the underdog (that would be me) spots the girl of his dreams but is savvy enough to know that's all she'll ever be.

Her honey-gold wavy hair peeks out from under a woollen hat, framing her face. The thick overcoat she wears only adds to her elegant appearance – like she's just stepped off a catwalk.

Megan... That's not her name but the nickname I've given her because, despite her blonde hair, she reminds me of a classy Megan Fox.

I try to speak, but my tongue feels like it's glued to the roof of my mouth. All I manage is a pathetic eyebrow raise. The last two times I tried to speak to this paragon of beauty, I made a complete ass of myself – a simple "Good morning" turning into a mix of mutism and stammering. *Oh, God* – just the memory of it makes my cheeks burn.

"Good morning, Kevin," she says like she's just passing me in the office and hasn't flown five thousand miles to be here. That, and she knows my name. *She knows my fucking name!*

"Hey Me...Me...gillie. Billie." I quickly clear my throat.

She cocks her head, a soft, amused smile playing on her lips. My stomach does a somersault. "W...what's going on?" I blurt out, immediately cringing at my own lame question.

She steps closer, and I'm instantly engulfed by her perfume – fresh, sweet, and utterly distracting. "Are you okay?" she asks, her voice laced with concern. "You're sweating." My hands fidget nervously at my sides.

"Yeah, cool... I'm good. I, um." I look around, desperate for a distraction. "How... did you get here?" *You gorgeous thing.*

"Rental," she smiles, turning to look across the lake. "I took a wrong turn, ended up at that burnt-down place over there. So I took it as an opportunity to explore. There's a trail through the woods that leads right here."

"Oh," is all I can say because I had no clue, and well, I'm in awe of her.

She observes me with a curious expression before turning to the work crew, breaking into a pearly white smile that defies the dark skies overhead. "You must be Irvin," she says warmly. "I've heard so many good things about you and your work. And this must be your crew..." She shakes more hands, and for a moment, it looks like she might actually hug these strangers like long-lost friends. Instead, she embarks on an all-out charm offensive.

She starts by complimenting England, talking about how it's always felt like a second home since she attended Oxford, how she loves afternoon tea, and how the English countryside is absolutely breathtaking. She even throws in a few lines about how she's always admired the English work ethic – how precise and dedicated people are, especially when it comes to preserving history and architecture.

Then she shifts gears. She's full of smiles and admiration, praising Irvin and his crew for their incredible work on the manor, their attention to detail, and their respect for the building's heritage – something she's never seen before in her entire career in property.

I watch as the tension in Irvin and the lads visibly melts away under her praise. It's like she's casting a spell on them, leaving them no choice but to nod in agreement as she gushes about how excited she is to have them on board for the final leg of the renovations.

I can't help but be in awe – and maybe a little envious. Where I fumbled and floundered, Billie has swooped in and smoothed everything over with ease. She's got the charm, the poise, and the perfect words to turn the whole situation around, leaving me feeling like I'm just along for the ride.

Fifteen minutes later, we're discussing the project in detail. Over the coming weeks, Frost Lake Manor will transform into a hive of activity. Irvin and his crew will collaborate with Karlson Fitouts, a division of Karlson Properties specialising in renovating historic estates into modern luxury hotels.

Karlson Fitouts will handle the major infrastructure upgrades, ensuring the manor meets modern standards and is equipped with state-of-the-art amenities. They'll also oversee the interior design, creating an ambiance that blends the manor's history with contemporary luxury. Additionally, they'll manage staffing, ensuring the hotel runs smoothly once it opens.

Irvin and his team will focus on preserving the manor's unique character throughout the renovations. It's an ambitious undertaking, but with careful collaboration, Frost Lake Manor should be ready to welcome guests by New Year's.

An hour later, numb from the biting wind, I secure Irvin & Sons' commitment, contingent on Battista's approval and doubling their crew. As they drive away, I realise, for the first time, a sense of excitement about this project.

And it's all thanks to one person.

She huddles into her coat, turning toward me with a smile that could melt ice. "I am freezing," she declares, hands buried deep in her pockets. "Can we please go get lunch before I lose a limb?"

"Billie..." I begin, trying to gather my thoughts.

"I know, I know. I'm sorry I took over back there. I didn't mean to go on for so long, but they seemed quite receptive, so I thought, *Strike while the iron is hot* and all that. And they only have one dealbreaker."

"Right. What's that?"

"They start early, leave early. No evening or night shifts."

"No evening or night shifts? That doesn't sound creepy at all."

She laughs, but I'm not joking.

"That was a great start," she says.

I want to stay on the subject of their dealbreaker, but her beautiful smile is disarming. Instead, I find myself saying, "You were amazing."

"Yeah?"

"Yes," I reply, and I mean it.

"Aw, thanks." Her smile widens, but I can see she's gauging my reaction.

So I get straight to it. "What are you doing here, Billie?" I ask, dread creeping into my voice. "Did your father send you?"

Her smile falters, eyes narrowing slightly. "My dad? Here? No. God, no." She shakes her head, her expression softening with amusement. "Would you believe me if I said I was here on vacation?"

I give her a pointed look.

She shrugs, self-aware. "Alright, you got me. I just thought you could use some help. You know, with marketing this place as you build up to the grand opening," she says, almost sheepishly. "And I happen to know a thing or two about that stuff. Even have a few contacts," she adds with a grin.

This isn't news to me – or to anyone in our business. Billie's an excellent public relations officer for the very reason she just showed. She's got that proverbial gift of the gab, and the way those smooth Texan vowels roll off her tongue makes her seem relatable, approachable. But don't be fooled. She knows exactly what she's saying and why. Many have underestimated her, only to fall foul of her stealthy skill.

"Which is why," I counter, "it'd make perfect sense for your dad to send you here. You know, keep an eye on me, make sure I don't screw up."

"Daddy didn't need to send me here, Kevin. He's already taken care of that," she says, her smile fading slightly.

"What do you mean?"

"Well, you've worked for him for the best part of a year. You know his motto, right?"

"Hard to miss. He's got a banner on his wall."

"*Action taken. Confidence restored,*" she says, her Texan drawl making the words sound almost like a mantra. "I've heard it since kindergarten. And he's taken action, Kevin."

"You mean by firing Jeremy?"

"By promoting you."

I cock my head because it sounds like a compliment but doesn't quite feel like one. "You know how we've been trying to get traction here for a while and how Jeremy found this place a few years back but failed to close. That was a major embarrassment for Daddy. And then..." she trails off here. I have no idea why other than to make sure I'm following.

I take my cue. "...and then," I continue. "the realtor reached out to me when it came back onto the market, and I—"

"And you took it to Daddy."

I nod. "Yeah. So?"

"Well, you're now my daddy's chance to redeem himself."

"I don't follow."

"When Jeremy failed to close, Daddy had to adjust his forecast. Made him look bad."

"He fired Jeremy out of revenge?"

"He fired Jeremy to show he'd taken action."

She pauses, letting the weight of her words sink in. A cold lump forms in my stomach, unease creeping up my spine. "He canned Jeremy to make himself look good?"

"No. Daddy fired Jeremy to cover his ass," she replies, voice steady, though there's a flicker of sympathy in her eyes. "He took action. He can't afford to make that mistake again. He wants a seat at the table."

"So, why hire me? Wouldn't it make sense to handle this himself?"

She hesitates. "Not really. He knows you're going to fail – no offence..."

I tilt my head. "Um, that actually sounds pretty offensive to me."

"He's hedging his bets. If you fail, he still looks like the tough guy who fired Jeremy and put his next best guy – at least on paper – on it. Because, for all intents and purposes, you're still a rookie."

"Easy with the compliments, I'm misting up here."

"If you fail, he'll swoop in come New Year's after you've done all the work and sign off on it. He'll look like the hero, and you'll look—"

"Fired." She gives me a weak smile. "Action taken. Confidence restored," I say, the lump in my throat sinking lower. I've always been in awe of the guy – even before I started there – so I didn't see any of this coming. Then again, why would I? The man gave me such a compelling speech when he handed me the project, I believed it was a genuine opportunity.

The sky grumbles overhead, reverberating around us. I want to ring him and tell him exactly where to shove his shitty job, but instead, I find myself asking, "So what are you doing here?"

My beautiful colleague, daughter of my new nemesis, has already turned to admire the building. "Huh?"

"You heard me, Billie. If you think I'm such a failure, why are you here?" I ask, struggling to keep the venom out of my voice.

She turns, eyes brimming with sincerity, and smiles. "I'm here because I think you're one hell of an agent."

"Yeah? How would you know?"

"I follow your work."

Whoa. I think my heart just stopped. "You do?"

"Of course."

Now it's restarted at double speed. "I didn't think you even knew I existed," I say, suddenly feeling like a teenager again.

She giggles. "That's funny. Because I felt the same."

I giggle too. And yes, it's a giggle – not even boyish, but a churlish combination of sounds followed by me awkwardly swallowing on a dry throat. "You're kidding, right?" I ask, trying to recover.

She shakes her head, and for a second, I notice something in her expression – a flicker of hesitation, maybe even nerves. *Wait... is she as nervous as I am? Don't be stupid. She's way out of your league.* But still...

Before I have time to process the thought, she quickly changes the subject. "How much do you know about this place?" she asks, turning back to the building.

I'm grateful for the shift. "Fifty acres of its own parkland, seventeen thousand square feet—"

"No. Not the property itself. Its history."

I pause, thrown by the question. "You mean the accident a few weeks ago? The woman who fell through the skylight and died?"

She gives me a look, the kind that says there's more to this story than I've been told.

"Yeah, I've read about that. The owner's wife, right? Marco Battista. He's had a rough time. His son dead, that house collapsing into the ocean – creepy stuff. It's all over the internet, and he even wrote a book about it."

She nods. "Right. But that's just part of it. There's more... going back to the people who lived here before him."

I scowl. "Are you trying to make me feel better or worse? Because right now, I'm leaning toward worse."

She ignores my comment. "You know, in the US, they have rules about disclosing deaths in a house. California, for example, requires sellers to reveal deaths that occurred within three years. But here in the UK? No such law. No need to disclose that sort of thing for homes... or hotels."

I raise an eyebrow. "You're suggesting we suppress what happened here?"

"No, I'm suggesting we shout it from the rooftops," she says, turning to me, eyes bright. "Do you have any idea how many millions of dollars in free publicity this place has already received?" It's rhetorical. "Then, we up the ante. We don't just brand this as another boring country hotel but an experience destination. People will flock here from all over the world, especially because of that book."

"The book isn't about this place, though. It's about his other home by the ocean."

"Technicality," she says, clearly thinking ahead, her sapphire eyes full of excitement.

I chuckle. "Yeah, I bet your father would have a lot to say about that."

But when I glance back, she isn't laughing. She's grinning, her face glowing with excitement.

"Oh, fuck. You're serious," I say, losing my smile.

"Of course I'm serious."

"Don't you think you should run this past your dad first?"

"What, like he was honest and aboveboard with you about this?" she asks, raising a brow.

"Yeah, but that's my problem, Billie, not yours. I don't want to stir up trouble between you and him."

"Are you kidding?" She shrugs. "It'd be just another chapter in our melodrama."

"And what about... Dave?"

She frowns, "Dave?"

"Yeah, David. Won't he have something to say about this?"

"Uh, yeah," she scoffs, "but why should I care?"

"Well, he's your... your, um," I falter, watching her brow lift again as I stumble over the words. "You two, um, you know... together."

She cringes. "Ew, what? Why would you think that?"

My stomach drops, the excitement of what I might be learning making my heart race. "Well, he's handsome in that captain-of-the-football-team kind of way, and he and your dad, they seem... you know... tight."

"Tight? Maybe. But that has nothing to do with me and everything to do with him being the son my dad always wanted," she says, shrugging.

"Seriously?"

"Yeah. Why do you think my name's Billie? He picked it before I was even born. And with Mom gone, well... it stuck." She says it casually, but I can see the sadness behind her eyes, a quiet longing. And I get it. I was raised on my aunt's farm, so I know what it's like to lose out on the life you thought you'd have.

"Oh, I'm sorry."

"Don't be." She steps closer, her perfume lingering in the wind. Her expression turning serious again. "Look, I know my dad. He's tough and smart, but he's also predictable. He thinks he's got everything under control, but there's one thing he didn't count on."

"What's that?" I ask, my voice barely a whisper.

"Me." She gives a small, confident smile. "I'm here because I believe in this project – and in you. Together, we can pull this off and beat him at his own game."

"So... what's the plan?" I ask, finally finding my voice.

She grins, that confident Billie I admire re-emerging. "First, we get this place ready for its grand debut. Then, we build the buzz – make Frost Lake

Manor the destination next year." There's a fire in her eyes, a determination that's contagious. And for the first time since I arrived, I feel like maybe, just maybe, I'm not as alone in this as I thought.

"So," she says, hunching against the cold. "Are you going to show me to my room?"

"Room?" I echo as dry leaves tumble and click around us.

"Yes. You know, so I can freshen up, maybe grab something to eat."

"Sure. I'm staying at a B&B not far from here. It's actually quite cute—"

"B&B? Why aren't you staying here?"

"Here?"

"Yes. Here."

I scoff. "You can't stay here."

"Why not?"

"Because... it isn't ready, and there's a gigantic hole in the roof."

"That's not what Irvin said. He mentioned the whole right side of the building is finished – multiple bedrooms with en suites, a family bathroom, a reception room, and the kitchen. Makes sense to try our own product."

"Yeah, but not in sub-zero temperatures."

She laughs. "Oh, quit ya gripin'. Just think of it as glampin'."

"Glamping? Have you been in there?"

"No, but how bad can it be?"

"Billie—"

"Come on, let's see this beauty," she says, heading toward the front door.

As I follow her, my phone buzzes in my pocket. The screen lights up with an unknown number, the area code unmistakably from Dallas. My stomach tightens – a call from the office. I hesitate, thumb hovering over the screen, but Billie catches sight of it and frowns.

"Don't," she says, more firmly than I expected.

"It could be important," I argue, though a part of me is relieved when she shakes her head.

"If it was important, they'd be calling from a number you recognise, right?"

I glance at the number again. She has a point. The last thing I want is to get sucked back into work drama, especially when the shadows of Frost Lake Manor are already creeping into my thoughts. I decline the call and slide the phone back into my pocket with a nod. "Yeah, you're right."

Frost Lake Manor is, quite literally, a house divided. The right side, as Billie described, is pristine – almost unnervingly so. This time, I allow my attention to wander beyond the devastation of the collapsed glass ceiling to the rest of the building. It's like stepping into a five-star hotel. The Battista crew really has done an impressive job – polished wood and gleaming fixtures everywhere. The walls are freshly painted, and despite the dust from the collapse, the floors are resplendent – where they aren't covered in mud and debris – reflecting the last of the autumn light streaming through the large windows.

On the right side of the staircase, each bedroom is immaculate, waiting only for the final touch – furniture to make them feel lived in. We wander through the rooms, and though most are empty, the smell of fresh paint and timber still lingers. One room stands apart. It has a bed, plainly made with now musty white sheets and a duvet. A small bedside table with a brass lamp casts a warm glow that pushes back the encroaching gloom. The room even has its own electric heater, which, when switched on, spreads a cocoon of warmth almost immediately. This room, with its views of the dense woodland and the lake beyond, must have been Marco Battista's.

But across the first landing and up the stairs, it's a completely different world – abandoned to the ravages of time. The air here is thick, oppressive, heavy with the scent of decay... and something else. Something I can't quite identify, like it crawled here to die and was never found.

The walls are faded, peeling, and the floors creak underfoot, groaning in protest at our presence. Dust coats every surface, and the temperature drops noticeably – the warmth from the other side of the house can't reach this far. Above us, giant plastic dust sheets hang from the ceiling, draped over banisters and stairs like shrouds. They move ever so slightly, a faint crinkling sound filling the silence, invisible drafts making them seem as though they're breathing – alive, yet suffocated, like the last remnants of life this side of the house once held.

I glance at Billie, and for once, she's uncharacteristically quiet. Her earlier bravado has dimmed, her eyes scanning the shadowed corners. I wonder if she feels it too – the weight of this place. I'm probably just projecting, letting last night's events and this unsettling environment mess with my head.

While I stop short of saying it aloud, I'm relieved when the tour ends and we're back on the brighter side of the house. Though I still can't say I'm thrilled about staying here overnight. Right now, the idea seems only marginally better than returning to the cramped B&B with its too-soft mattress... and the memory of that nightmare.

So, when Billie suggests we go out for supplies and takeout, I jump at the chance.

Fawnham is larger than Fawndale, but still not too far from the manor, and the drive is a welcome break. The normalcy of the town's bustle is a stark contrast to the eerie silence of the manor. I've barely parked and killed the engine when my phone buzzes again, the same unknown number from Dallas flashing on the screen.

"Shit," I mutter, picking it up.

Billie glances over, her expression tightening. "Don't answer it," she repeats. "Important calls don't come from unrecognised numbers."

I'm not sure I agree, but she has a point. If it were someone truly important – like Anderson – their name would show up. So I silence the call, and we leave the car.

We pick up an inflatable bed for me – after my insistence that Billie take the bedroom – along with assorted groceries and Chinese takeout from a hole-in-the-wall place that smells far too good to pass up.

By the time we return to Frost Lake Manor, the sun is already sinking, the golden light of late afternoon fading into the creeping shadows of dusk. The birds have vanished as if retreating before the encroaching night, leaving the air still. Even the wind has stopped, as though the whole world is holding its breath.

On the bright side, the manor is fully lit. Power still runs to the place, casting long shadows across the devastation of the lobby. But the heating? A no-go. No matter how many switches we flip, the radiators remain cold and silent.

We decide to settle in the main bedroom, giving it a quick clean. The room is thick with cobwebs, but Billie barely blinks as she clears them away, banishing the occasional spider to the trash. After dusting and tidying, we close the door to the drafty hallway and turn on the electric heater.

With no table, I spread a blanket on the floor and lay out the food containers and bottles of water, setting up a makeshift picnic. I place a battery-powered lantern in the centre, casting a warm glow over our spread. The food isn't hot anymore, but the savoury smell is a welcome change from the cold, musty air that seems to cling to every corner of the manor.

"Wow," Billie says, emerging from the bathroom, followed by another cloud of her perfume. "This looks great."

"Madam," I reply, gesturing to the picnic on the floor. "I'm just going to wash my hands. Be right back. Are you sure you don't want me to run you over to pick up your car and things?"

"No. Really. I'm fine. I have everything I need for tonight."

"Are you sure?"

She nods, enthusiastically, "I'm sure."

The scent in the bathroom is even stronger, thick in the confined space, catching in the back of my throat. I quickly wash my hands, coughing as I dry them with paper towels. I hurry out, closing the door behind me – something about that fragrance is making me queasy.

Billie's sitting cross-legged on the blanket. "Come, take a seat," she says, smiling.

I'm about to join her when something catches my eye beyond the window. Darkness has swallowed the land. Where there was once autumnal colour, now a legion of twisted tree silhouettes stretch out like skeletal limbs. The air feels unnaturally still. I glance up to see the moon rising, casting a ghostly glow on the lake. The surface is like a mirror, reflecting the cold, star-studded sky. At the far end, near the remains of the burnt-down house, a patch of fog has appeared, ebbing and flowing like it's alive, slowly creeping across the water toward us.

"Huh, that's weird," I say, squinting.

"What is?" Billie asks.

"A fog's rolling in," I say, still staring into the gloom.

"Oh, that happens a lot here. It's not unusual," she says casually.

"Yeah, but this one's moving like... like dry ice, but there's no wind," I mutter, cupping my hand to the glass for a better look. "It's coming from that place on the other side. I wonder what happened there."

"The fire?"

"You know about that?"

"Of course. It was supposed to be a happy day – lots of love and joy. But that changed once the fire started."

I turn around. "What happened?"

"It's hard to know," she says, casually unwrapping food containers. "There are so many rumours, but most people believe it was one of Marco Battista's disgruntled patients."

"Patients?"

"Yeah, didn't you know? He's a psychologist."

"No, I thought he was a property developer."

"He is, but he was renting that place while buying this one. Things didn't go as planned."

"So... what, she set the fire during the wedding?"

Billie pauses, looking up. "She set *herself* on fire. According to him, she uttered some kind of curse."

"Oh, my God." I grimace, picturing the chaos – the screams, the smell.

I glance back out the window, half-expecting to see it play out. "That's horrendous," I whisper. "Why would she do that?"

Billie shrugs, unfazed. "Different stories. Some say she was crazy. Others think it was revenge for him kicking her out of her home."

"Her home?"

"Yeah, here at Frost Lake Manor – at least, that's what Battista told the police, though they never found her body." Billie's words are casual, like it's just gossip.

"You don't believe him?" I ask.

Another shrug. "The mind's a terrifying thing," she says, her voice lowering. "It can make us see things that aren't even there."

The fog has spread across the lake, swallowing the dock and creeping over the lawn.

"Wow... that fog's a lot closer now," I mutter, squinting as it slinks toward the building like tendrils. A shiver runs down my spine as I remember last night. I hesitate as I consider what I'm about to say next. "I think *I* saw something," I blurt. "Something that wasn't there."

My eyes meet hers, realising too late I should've kept my mouth shut. Now I feel weird – part of me comfortable with her, but the other part... well, I don't want to sound like an idiot.

"Something?" she asks, her gaze steady.

"Yeah, last night. I could've imagined it, but it felt like someone was there. At the B&B."

"Inside your room?"

"No." I shake my head. "Outside. Right by my door."

She cocks her head. "What were they doing?"

"That's the thing. I don't know."

"You don't know?"

I force a chuckle, trying to shrug it off. "No, just had this feeling, like someone was standing there."

"And they didn't say anything?"

"No." I nod, laughing awkwardly. "Yeah, it sounds stupid. It was raining, and... well, it just creeped me out. And this morning..." I trail off, regretting I've said this much.

"This morning?" she prompts.

"It doesn't matter," I mumble.

"No, come on. You started this. Tell me."

I sigh. "This morning, I found something outside my door."

"Something?" she asks.

"Yeah, a ball. About the size of a baseball but made of... vine and thorns." I force a laugh. "I know, it sounds crazy," I say, expecting her to laugh. But she doesn't. Her amused smile has vanished, replaced by something much more... serious.

"What?" I ask, suddenly uneasy. "What is it?"

She hesitates, clearly weighing whether to tell me. "It's nothing. Just... more urban legend."

"Too late for that. You've got to tell me now."

She shakes her head. "It's just a story. Something that happened a few years back. In Cambridge."

"Massachusetts?"

"No, here in England. A small village just outside the city. Meadow Lane, I think it was called." She pauses, taking a breath. "There were reports of some really bad stuff happening there. Messed-up stuff. People died, and..."

"And?" I press, unease twisting in my gut.

"And... some of the victims, they found these little effigies. Shaped like a ball."

It takes me a second to process what she's saying. Then... I laugh, starting small, more confused than anything. But as it builds, I catch myself wondering if she's joking. When Billie laughs too, a flood of relief washes over me, and I join in more heartily, pointing at her. "Ha, you're good! You're... really good," I say, laughing harder. "You almost had me there!"

The laughter lingers a bit too long. Maybe because, for a moment, she really did have me crapping my pants. But it fades when a creaking noise sounds behind me. I freeze, my eyes snapping to the window.

The fog has swallowed the mansion, pressing itself against the glass like it's alive – thick and swirling. It moves with intent, gliding over the surface, almost like it's testing the windows for weaknesses.

I watch, heart thumping, as it curls around the edges of the frame, making the glass creak under the pressure. For a second, I swear I see it pulse – almost like it's... breathing.

Suddenly, my pocket vibrates.

"Shit!" I yelp, nearly jumping out of my skin. Fumbling, I grab my phone, hands shaking. The screen lights up with that same unrecognised number – the Dallas area code glaring back at me.

"It's that number again," I mutter, but this time, I don't wait for Billie to talk me out of it. I hit answer and hold the phone to my ear.

"Hello?"

Nothing. Dead air for a few seconds, then a rush of static, followed by a sharp squeal that makes me wince. I yank the phone away and shout into it, "Hello? Can you hear me?"

Hiss. Static. Squeal.

"I can't hear you! Whoever you are, hang up and try again." I'm about to end the call when a voice finally comes through – one I recognise instantly.

...Hello? Can you hear me? Hello? Kevin, is that you?

My stomach drops.

Slowly, phone in hand, I turn to look at Billie, who's still sitting there, legs folded, casually eating.

"Billie?" I stammer, barely managing to speak.

"Yeah?" says the person sitting in front of me – but so does the voice on the phone!

Static crackles.

...Yeah, I've been trying to reach you. I'm on my way to the manor, but my GPS isn't working. Can you give me directions?

The world tilts. This can't be real. It doesn't make any sense.

A loud, splitting noise pulls my attention to the window. I whirl around – the windowpane is cracked! But before I can process it, something else catches my eye. The fog is shifting, peeling apart like it's revealing something. Something that shouldn't be there. And yet, as the mist swirls in the windowlight, they come into view – crude and ragged, just like the ones by the road.

Scarecrows.

They're lined up on the lawn, heads crooked, shadows stretching their jagged forms across the ground. Their burlap faces droop, hollow and lifeless, as they watch the house. Watch *me.*

"JESUS CHRIST! Billie!" I spin away from the window. "Billie, they're here! They're—"

I stop mid-sentence.

The blanket, the containers, and the half-eaten food are still there, but Billie is gone. The bedroom door hangs wide open.

"Billie?" I call out, scanning the room even though I can already see I'm alone. "Billie?!"

I shout toward the bathroom, but deep down, I know she isn't there. I take a step forward, but the air feels heavier, thick with a sickly-sweet scent – her perfume, but underneath it, something else... something rotten. It's subtle at first, but then it hits me, harder now, like damp earth and decay, something long hidden.

I gag, bile rising in my throat.

The phone in my hand crackles with static again, then goes dead.

I stumble back, panic rising in my chest as the room grows colder, like the fog is seeping through every crack.

"Billie?" It's barely a whisper, a reflex, as I try to make sense of this. *We see what we want to see.* Her words echo in my mind, crawling under my skin. The stench left behind thickens, choking me.

I need to get out of here. Now.

I take a step toward the door but freeze when the bedside lamp flickers and sputters – then dies. A second later, the corridor light goes out, too. The house plunges into darkness. Panic crawls up my legs, tightening around my chest.

If it weren't for the lantern on the blanket, the room would be swallowed by the dark. Its warm glow is the only thing keeping the blackness at bay. I reach for it but stop. I see movement.

At first, I think it's just a trick of the light, but then I see it again. Something is moving.

The once-silent house groans around me. Ancient timbers creak under invisible pressure. Outside, the wind picks up, rattling the windows, howling beneath the door.

My heart pounds as I squint at the blanket. My eyes adjust to the flickering gloom, and that's when I see it – something is crawling over it.

I blink, trying to make sense of it, but no... Oh, shit. It isn't a trick of the light. What I thought were noodles spilled from the takeout containers are now wriggling, slick and fast, scuttling forward from the food.

Spiders. Hundreds of them.

"FUCK!" I shriek, jumping back. But they keep coming, spilling across the blanket, legs scrambling in every direction. Their bloated black bodies surge toward me, moving as one writhing mass.

I take another step back, my breath catching, the cold from the window biting at the back of my neck.

BANG!

Something slams into the window behind me. Hard.

I whirl around, heart in my throat, face to face with it – a scarecrow, its burlap face pulling back before smashing into the glass again.

I scream.

The thing wails through a gash in its mouth, then jerks its head forward – *SMASH!* Again. And again. The sound is deep, hollow, like bones cracking against wood. A web of cracks splinters across the windowpane.

"NO!" I breathe, backing up fast.

The scarecrow's head lolls sideways, crooked. Its straw limbs twitch unnaturally as it hurls itself into the glass over and over. The window rattles, the frame splintering with each impact.

I tear my eyes away, holding the lantern up in front of me as I bolt for the door, ignoring the wet crunch of spider abdomens beneath my feet.

As I emerge in the dark corridor, the wind slams into me, howling through the gap in the roof. The tarp above snaps viciously, the sound like the jaws of a beast slamming shut, while plastic dust sheets flap violently, desperate to break free.

BANG!

Another loud crash echoes from down the hall – then another, and another, from different rooms. *SLAM! SLAM!* The sound is unmistakable – they're all trying to get inside.

The house groans under the assault. Doors rattle, and the ancient timber creaks and shudders under the invisible pressure. The wind outside shrieks, shaking the windows and clawing at the walls.

My heart pounds as I glance over the banister, trying to spot the front door through the darkness. But it's impossible to see if it's really there or if it's just burned into my memory. Either way, I have to reach it. I have to get out.

"SHIT!"

The grandfather clock – dead for so long, just a lifeless relic – suddenly chimes. Its haunting, warbled rendition of Big Ben's Westminster Quarters echoes through the chaos.

I thought that thing was dead.

The sound is deafening, even over the storm tearing the house apart, and its sound empties a bucket of ice-cold terror down my spine.

I step forward but kick something. It rolls out of the lantern's beam and tumbles down the stairs with a loud *plop! plop! plop!* The most terrifying part – the thing that makes my scalp prickle with sweat – is that I don't need to see it to know what it is.

I saw it at the hotel. I threw it in the trash.

Yet it's here now – *Oh, God.*

I lift the lantern higher, casting long, distorted shadows that rise and surround me. From below, that ugly thing stops tumbling, settling somewhere in the darkness.

I take a ragged breath. It's cold. So cold that my breath leaves my body in clouds of vapour.

Kevin…

I spin around. The sound is barely a whisper, drawn out like the last exhale of something that hasn't breathed in years, coming from the corridor to my right where the lantern's light fades into black. Billie? The voice sounded like hers – yet it didn't. It's too far away. Too wrong, like it's been stretched and twisted.

I peer into the gloom. The howling turbulence from the gaping hole above is loud, but the rest of the house is eerily quiet, like it's holding its breath.

"Billie?" My voice cracks, weak, swallowed by the shadows. I wait, staring into the void. Nothing stirs, but the raised hairs on my neck react to the feeling that something's down there, crouched just beyond the lantern's reach, waiting to lunge.

I take a step back, shivering, gaze locked on the corridor, waiting for the voice to call again. But it doesn't.

Crinkle.

Something moves across from me. I whip around, pulse pounding in my ears. The dust sheets are swaying as if something – no, someone – is brushing past them. That crinkling sound is sandpaper on my frayed nerves. I raise the lantern, holding it high toward the opposite side of the staircase.

Crinkle. Lift. Settle. The sheets shift, ghost-like, back and forth, as if the very house were breathing.

I inch forward carefully, toes feeling for the edge of the top step, lantern held high, straining to see beyond the sheets. There's something there. I'm sure of it. A shadow, right where—

KEVIN!

The rasping voice is sudden, sharp in my right ear. I yelp, jumping sideways, miscalculating the step. Before I know it, the world tilts. My body slams into the stairs, the lantern flying from my hand, clattering loudly as I tumble head over heels, each bone-rattling impact knocking the wind from my lungs. The sky and hard steps spin in my vision – up, down, sideways – until everything goes black.

When I come to, my head is swimming, my cheek pressed awkwardly against the cold wood of the stairs. I've no clue how long I've been out, but my body is aching from the fall, and I'm shivering. It's so bad that my teeth are chattering, and I can barely feel my fingers. *Or maybe that's from the tumble too – hard to tell.*

I clench my fists to test my strength, but a bolt of pain shoots through me, and I cry out. Still, I try again, forcing my limbs to respond. I need to move. I need to get out of here.

The lantern's dead, broken from the fall. The landing is steeped in darkness, punctuated only by faint moonlight filtering down from the hole in the ceiling. But it's weak, barely there. I lie immobilised as clouds shift, periodically blocking the light and plunging everything into pitch black. Then, the moonlight reappears in narrow, pale strips, and the cycle repeats itself.

My mind wants to move, but the pain in my body begs me to lie here, listening to the gale buffeting overhead, howling through the corridors. *You're going to die here. Get up. Now!*

I'm considering this when I hear another sound, barely audible at first but growing louder. At first, I think it's me, fearing I may have seriously injured myself. But when I move my arms, I can't recreate the noise. Then, just when I think I'm imagining it, there it is again.

Click... pop... click... pop.

I strain my ears, trying to locate it. The moonlight flickers out, and I'm swallowed by darkness.

Click... pop.

It's growing louder. Closer.

I push myself up onto my elbows, pulse racing, squinting into the blackness. Something's moving, crawling toward me, but I can't see it. Just a ghostly white shape edging closer.

Moonlight floods back in.

Nothing.

Then darkness again.

Click... pop... click... pop.

Panic surges through me. I fumble for the phone in my pocket, praying it wasn't damaged in the fall. My fingers, cold and shaky, finally grasp it. I tap on the screen... nothing. Come on... I tap again, harder this time. Still nothing.

Click! Pop! Click! Pop!

Faster now. Closer. Too close.

"Turn on flashlight!" I croak, my voice scraping in my throat. "Turn on!"

Turning on flashlight.

The phone's beam flickers to life, a narrow shaft cutting through the darkness. For a second, I see nothing but the opposite wall, the dust sheets shifting slightly in the draft.

Then the beam moves.

And I see it. *Oh, God. Help me.*

It starts with the rag – tattered, stained, a mockery of white. Then the limbs, pallid and impossibly contorted, emerge like the legs of some nightmare arachnid. It scuttles toward me, head twisted back, ceiling-ward, in a grotesque parody of supplication.

But it's the eyes that steal my breath. Dead white, glassy, they glint unblinkingly in the cold LED glow of my phone, framed by strands of long limp white hair.

I try to scream, but my throat locks. Frozen, I watch in horror as the creature closes the distance. Six feet... five... four... long, bony fingers, tipped with jagged black nails, reach for my ankles. I jerk my feet away, heart hammering, but the thing keeps advancing.

Closer. Faster.

Click! Pop! Click! Pop!

A bone-chilling scream rips through the room, and I realise that it's mine. The thing reacts, its jaw unhinging, distending wider than humanly possible. The screech that follows is a tearing, unnatural sound, like metal scraping against bone. The stench that comes with it is so foul, I gag.

My phone slips from my numb fingers, the light beam dancing wildly as it falls, casting grotesque shadows across the walls.

The moonlight shifts. Darkness engulfs me.

And in the suffocating blackness, the only sound is the slow, relentless *click... pop... click... pop*, echoing like a macabre metronome counting down to an unspeakable fate.

I don't hesitate. I jump to my feet, grab my stricken phone, and stumble down the remaining steps. Legs wobbling, I race blindly for the front door, rip it open, and plunge through it into the night.

Freezing air welcomes me, but I don't stop – adrenaline driving me toward my car.

The clouds have parted now; the moon is shining bright. There's no creepy mist. No scarecrows. Just the cold biting at my skin and a stilled world with a quiet so normal, I feel like I want to cry.

I slam up against the car, gasping for air, my breaths sharp and cutting. It's okay. You're safe. But the thought feels hollow as I glance back at the house, expecting that thing to burst through the door at any moment.

Nothing.

Minutes crawl by and still nothing. My chest heaves, heart thundering, as I clutch my phone like a lifeline. Did that really happen? Of course, it did – didn't it?

The lights are back on, spilling that soft amber glow as if everything's fine. As if I hadn't just been chased by a nightmare.

An owl hoots nearby, snapping me back. My arm aches from the fall. That was real. But was the rest?

Who gives a shit? I'm out of here!

I frisk my pockets for the car keys. There is no way I'm—

What was that?

I spin around. I heard something. A voice. Out there. In the woods. I lift my phone, its beam revealing a narrow path, leading off the courtyard and into the skeletal trees and – *Oh, shit!*

A light. A flashlight, flickering among giant tree trunks.

"Hello?" I call out, the word escaping into the night.

It's deathly quiet out here – so quiet I can hear the ringing in my ears.

"Hello?" I repeat, my voice barely more than a whisper.

I wait... nothing.

Then, a short, sharp cry. *Not a person, you idiot. A fox.*

But that doesn't explain the light projecting giant shadows into the sky.

A flashlight?

"Billie?" I call, louder this time. "Billie? Is that you?"

Still nothing. Just that light, bobbing in the distance, weaving through the trees. I take a step toward the woods, every instinct screaming at me to just get in the damn car.

But... what if it's her? I can't abandon her out here.

Here... Over here.

I freeze in my tracks. I heard that. I definitely heard that. A voice – a loud whisper – hesitant, yet desperate, calling out from the dark.

I take another step. Then another. The trees loom larger the closer I get, the light barely visible through thickening shadows.

"Billie?" I shout again. "Is that you?" But my voice is swallowed by the cold.

I'm halfway to the treeline when I hear it again.

A voice.

Her voice.

Kevin... Help me!

It's faint, but I hear it. Clear as day. She's calling for me.

"Billie!" I shout, breaking into a jog, heading straight for the woods. She's out there. She needs me.

I stray off the courtyard and into the woods, following the footpath cutting through the trees. But I'm not stupid – at least, I don't think I am. I stop about ten feet in, keeping the car in view – my ticket out of here that I don't dare lose sight of.

Moonlight filters through the trees in fragmented shafts, revealing the outlines of gnarled trunks and elongated branches. My breath fogs out into the light beam of my phone, each exhale louder than the last.

"BILLIE!" I call out again, eyes locked on the small light flickering deeper in the woods.

Kevin... Kevin, is that you? Her voice reaches me again, weak but distinct, cutting through the silent forest like a blade.

"YES! Billie, it's me! Come towards me! Follow my voice!"

I strain my eyes, watching the light flicker and sway, bobbing up and down as she moves toward me. I can hear her now. Footsteps crunching through the underbrush. Warm relief floods through me. She's picked up the pace, hurrying toward me, that small light growing larger as she draws closer and closer.

"That's it! Follow my voice!" I shout, panic slowly subsiding.

I glance back towards the safety of the car.

Something shifts in the corner of my eye. I turn and see another light flickering on the opposite side of the woods. Then, a third. They're weaving through the trees. I freeze, heart pounding, glancing between the bobbing light ahead and the others moving in from the side. They're circling, closing me in. Then I hear it – a low hum that quickly turns into the rumble of an engine. Headlights cut through the darkness, stretching and shrinking around tree trunks, creating a dizzying radial effect. Tires scrunch on gravel as the vehicle comes to a stop behind mine.

Thank God. Somebody's here.

"Billie, somebody's—" Relief dies as quickly as it came when I turn back to the light in the trees.

It's no longer a light.

It's *mist!* The same mist from before, creeping along the ground, twisting around the tree trunks like a living thing. It slithers through the air, moving with purpose, gliding toward me – thick and unnatural. I back up instinctively, the cold sinking into my bones as my breath catches in my throat.

I raise my phone, holding up the light and squinting into the fog, trying to make out what's ahead. But the beam doesn't do anything. It's as if the light is being devoured by the mist, swallowing it whole.

Billie? Billie? Is that you? The sound freezes the blood in my veins. It's a voice, calling out from inside the mist. One that I instantly recognise... It's mine. At least it sounds like me. The sound is loud, uncanny, like I'm listening to a recording of myself – distorted, warped – calling out from all directions.

B...Billie... BILLIE... Is that you? Is that you? The voice asks, the intonation shifts with every repetition, the voice testing different tones and pitches, like it's learning how to speak. Slower now. *"Is... that... YOU? Billie?"*

Hot and cold shivers rake through me. Something out there is mimicking me.

Billie... BILLIE... Billie...Is that you?

Suddenly, the phone in my hand vibrates, the screen lighting up. I jump, almost dropping it, but manage to hold on. I gape at the screen – it reads BILLIE ANDERSON. My heart thunders in my chest as I press the answer button.

There's a burst of static, and then... *What's that? Voices?* Faint at first... no, not voices – whispering, drifting, like smoke out of the speaker and filling the air around me.

"Billie?" I croak.

The incoherent whispers continue, rising and falling in volume for several seconds. I instinctively lean in closer before the whispering stops abruptly and a voice I don't recognise rasps *THIS IS WHERE YOU END.*

Then, there's an ear-splitting sound – like metal scraping – before the screen flickers out.

SNAP! Movement nearby. It was just a shadow, but I saw it! I saw it! One of those trees just moved! It just fucking moved!

The mist surges forward as if searching for something... searching... for me!

I don't even think about it – I turn and bolt, racing back towards the house just as fingernails – cold as ice – brush the nape of my neck. I yelp, eyes glued to the safety of the vehicle as its brake lights flood the night with a deathly red glow.

"I'M HERE! I'M HERE!" I scream, my voice hoarse, throat raw. Branches lash at my face, thorns catch at my hands, but I tear through the underbrush toward the light – towards salvation.

And I'm almost there when the ground beneath me shifts, slick with mud, coagulated and thick like blood, and my foot catches on something – a root, a vine, I don't know – and I go down hard, face-first into the freezing muck.

I groan, pain shooting up my leg. But there's no time. No time! I push myself up, hands slipping in the mire, eyes fixed on the red brake lights before they flicker, then die.

"HELP! HELP ME!" I wail, my voice cracking, desperation clawing at my chest. Then, a faint clunk – the driver's door swings open. A booted heel hits the ground, and then another. And then—

It's Billie!

"BILLIE! BILL—" My shout is cut off by a sharp prick on my hand. I jerk it back with a hiss of pain, my gaze dropping to the ground. There, nestled in the mud, is one of those thorn balls – ugly, twisted, glistening under the faint moonlight.

Before I can process it, a cold, numbing sensation spreads from the prick, up my wrist. My muscles seize. Tight. Too tight. I try to scream, but the sound dies in my throat. My legs stiffen, then my arms, and finally my chest. The more I fight it, the worse it gets – the sensation of being pinned to the earth, suffocated by something unseen. My body is shutting down.

I look up. Billie is standing there, holding something to her ear. Seconds later, the mud vibrates, and my phone screen lights up the night. "HERE! I'M HE—"

My jaw clenches, locking shut. The paralysis crawls up my neck, choking me, spreading like poison, cold and relentless.

My feet solidify, then my legs, as the paralysis climbs higher, gripping my throat, making each breath shallower until I can't breathe. I can't breathe!

HELP! HELP ME! I scream, but it's only in my head.

The world swims, my vision blurring at the edges. I can't move! My head locks in place, stiff and unyielding. The only part of me still working is my eyes – wild with terror, rolling in their sockets.

I can only watch as Billie stands there, her woollen hat framing her oblivious face, eyes scanning the driveway, calling out into the night.

BILLIE! OVER HERE! OVER HERE! But she doesn't hear me. She can't.

My vision blurs again, and that's when I see it. Through the fog, something moves.

A figure shuffles forward, emerging from the mist, which parts as if in fear. I blink, and the vision sharpens. Ragged layers of fabric – a shawl, dark and tattered, barely concealing the grotesque, patchy skin beneath. Straw, twisted into something like a face, peers from behind strands of wiry white hair. The number 13 winks at me in the moonlight, pinned to her shawl.

But it can't be...

She's close now. The sucking sound of her feet – bare and twisted – in the mud is louder than my thudding heart. Roots and vines twine around her feet like she's growing out of the earth itself.

I try to react but can't. All I can do is watch as a gnarled, dirty hand reaches down, long fingers brushing my face before burlap – rough and cold – is pulled over my head and tightened around my neck.

Then... nothing.

Just silence.

JACKSON ANDERSON

NEW YEAR'S.

SEVERAL WEEKS LATER.

The hum of the central heating is the only sound breaking the silence in the luxurious suite. I lean back in the leather chair, a crystal tumbler of aged whiskey in hand, its rich aroma filling the air. Downstairs, the staff's scurrying around, putting the final touches on Frost Lake Manor for tonight's soft opening. But up here, it's just me, savouring the quiet before the night unfolds. The manor is finally ready. Hell, it's more than ready – it's a damn masterpiece. The destination for anyone who's anyone and my ticket to a seat on the board.

And to think, that snivelling kid Kevin almost derailed the whole thing. I knew he didn't have the balls for a project this size, but even I didn't expect him to bolt like a damn coward in the middle of the night.

My phone buzzes, and I glance down at the coffee table, a smile already spreading across my face. I tap answer and bring the phone to my ear.

"Hey, sweetheart," I say, leaning back and swirling the whiskey. "You on your way?"

Yeah, should be there in about thirty minutes.

"Good," I reply, taking a sip.

"How are things?"

"All good here, babe. Place looks fantastic. Floors, doors, everything's gleaming. Contractors did a hell of a job. And it's all thanks to you."

Thanks, Daddy, but it was a team effort.

"Horseshit, credit where it's due. If you hadn't stepped in, this place would've been a disaster. That asshole really screwed the pooch on this one, but you pulled it together. That's all on you, babe."

Still no word from him, then? She asks, voice softer this time.

I sigh, already feeling my blood heat. "You're still worried about this guy? Honey, I told ya. We're never gonna hear from him again. He bailed, and that's all there is to it. Now, I know that big heart of yours don't wanna hear it, but trust me – the guy's history."

There's a pause – longer this time, filled in by the sound of a cart and footsteps in the corridor outside.

Yeah... it's just... weird, you know? You've seen his work. This just doesn't feel like him.

"Well, you know what they say – some folks are all hat and no cattle." I keep my tone steady, trying to reel her back in. "And let me tell ya, if it wasn't for your idea to revise that letter of intent, we wouldn't even be here right now. You bought us the time we needed to get this place ready, hon. That was you."

I know, you're right... I just can't get over it. You know, the contractors saying they met with me that Monday. My flight hadn't even landed yet."

"Yeah, I know, honey, you said."

"Don't you think that's weird? And what about that night? First, I couldn't get through, then I found his abandoned rental out front...and I could've sworn I heard him call my name, Daddy. It was crystal clear, like I'm talking to you right now."

"Billie, honey, you've really gotta stop torturin' yourself like this. Now, as you well know, the cops found nothin'. No trace of the guy either at the house or in the woods... nothin'."

Exactly. Who disappears like that without so much as a text?

I shake my head, stifle a sigh. "Honey, you heard what the police said. He wasn't about to text anyone. The guy was a loner. And—"

But that's what bothers me, Daddy. There's no record of him even returning to the States. And after that phone call today...

Her words hang in the air, and I sit up, tension returning to my shoulders. "Phone call? What phone call? Have you heard from this asshole? Because if you have, then you damn well better tell the po—"

No, Daddy, nothing like that.

"Then what is it, hon?"

She hesitates, and I can hear the hum of her car in the background. She finally speaks. *It doesn't matter. It just worried me, is all.*

"You sure?"

Yeah. I'm sure.

I lean back in the chair, the warmth of the room sinking into my neck. For the first time in a long while, things feel... good. "Well, listen, doll, I need to jump and finish getting ready before you show up. We'll do that last-minute check together." I stretch, standing up, when there's a sudden knock at the door.

"Hang on a second, sweetheart," I say, frowning. "Someone's knockin' on the damn door."

I walk across the room, the floorboards creaking softly underfoot. As I reach for the handle, the air feels colder, almost biting, as I pull the door open...

But there's nobody there.

I glance down the corridor – it's empty. The hallway stretches out in both directions, dimly lit by the sconces flickering on the walls.

Who is it? comes Billie's voice through the phone, sharper now, like she's on edge. *Daddy?*

"Yeah, I'm here, honey."

Is everything okay?

"Yeah, fine," I say, rubbing the back of my neck. "Could've sworn someone knocked on my door, but there ain't nobody here."

I'm about to turn back inside when something at the edge of the light catches my eye.

"What the...?"

Daddy? Daddy, what is it?

It looks like a ball. It's sitting just outside the door, half-hidden in the shadows. I bend down, frowning as I pick it up. No bigger than a baseball, but it's... wrong. Twisted. Like it's made of vines or thorns, all tangled together. The surface is slick, wet from the rain, the thorns glistening under the dim light.

Daddy? What is it? Daddy, answer me.

"I'm here, honey. I'm here," I say into the phone, but my focus is on the ball. "It's the damnedest thing. Someone left this strange little ball outside my door."

What? What is it? Her voice cracks now, strain tightening each word.

"Now, settle down, sweetheart," I mutter, turning the thing in my hands. It's heavier than it looks. "Just... some ugly ball. Looks like it's got... what the hell... thorns all through it."

Daddy... listen to me... you need to get rid of it... right now.

"What?" I chuckle, shaking my head. "What're you getting yourself all het up about? It's just some dumb prank—"

Get rid of it! Her voice cracks into a shout. Daddy, please! Get rid of it now!

I glance at the ball again, but something flickers in the corner of my eye – one of the sconces on the wall.

"Oh, hell..."

What? What is it?

"The lights... they're actin' up." I watch the hallway as shadows seem to stretch and crawl along the walls. "Listen, doll, I gotta get someone on this. I'll see you soon, alright?"

No! Daddy, no! Don't hang up! Don't—

There's a burst of static in my ear, sharp and grating. I pull the phone away for a second, frowning, but then... Another sound... Not quite voices. Faint at first, like something's scratching at the edges, whispering, drifting through the speaker... Whispering.

"Billie? Is that you?"

The whispers rise and fall, incoherent but unsettling, filling the air around me. I listen closer, straining to make out the words. Then, everything stops – dead silent.

Before I can react, a voice rasps through the static, low and ragged, like it's crawling straight into my brain. *THIS... IS... WHERE YOU END.*

Then, the phone dies. The lights flicker out, plunging the corridor into suffocating darkness.

My breath catches, the air thick like molasses, choking me. I cough, gag, stumble, my brain screaming for oxygen. I can't breathe. I... can't breathe. Panic rises as the surrounding air tightens, trapping me, each breath harder than the last.

The corridor lights flicker, strobing in sync with the pounding of my heart. I claw my way forward, gasping, pleading. "H...H...e...l...p... m...e."

Lights flicker...

OFF... Darkness

ON... An empty corridor stretches endlessly before me. "H...elp."

OFF... A shadow jitters towards me.

ON... There's nothing there.

OFF... The walls are closing in.

ON... The shadow is much closer now, just feet away.

OFF... A rustle in the dark – closer!

ON... The flickering speeds up. My heart races, pounding so fast, I think it's going to explode.

OFF... Click! Pop! Click! Pop! Something stirring in the black.

ON... Elongated arms, twisted like branches, tipped with jagged talons, stretch toward me. Pain explodes in my chest as the talons sink deep. A sharp, sudden agony as my heart gives one final desperate beat before—

OFF...

Blackness.

ENJOYED THIS TERROR MORSEL?

If you enjoyed this short story, part of the Haunted universe, but it's left you wanting more, explore the complete series and see how the terrifying threads all come together, visit Tony's Amazon page. Or if you'd like to experience the chilling tale of The Curse of Frost Lake Manor in a whole new way, don't miss the exclusive adaptation on the world's #1 horror podcast, Dr. NoSleep. Available now on YouTube and all major podcast platforms.

THE #1 BESTSELLING
HAUNTED SERIES SO FAR...

Scan to visit Tony's Amazon page

FOLLOW TONY

If you can't wait for Tony Marturano's next thriller, subscribe to the blog, mailing list, or follow on social media for the latest news, special chapter previews and exclusive giveaways.

www.tonymarturano.com

JOIN THE MAILING LIST
visit www.tonymarturano.com,
click on contact and subscriptions.

LIKE THE FACEBOOK PAGE
facebook.com/tonymarturano.author

BROWSE INSTAGRAM
instagram.com/marturanotony

FOLLOW ON TWITTER
twitter.com/tmarturano

or google tony marturano

Printed in Great Britain
by Amazon

49538358R00040